BULL IN THE RING

A NOVEL

AL ORTOLANI

Meadowlark **PRESS**

Emporia, Kansas, USA

Meadowlark Press, LLC
PO BOX 333, Emporia, KS 66801
Meadowlark-books.com
Meadowlark Editor: Emilie A. Moll

Cover image: TMS & Emilie A. Moll

FICTION / Small Town & Rural
FICTION / Coming of Age
FICTION / Historical / General

Library of Congress Control Number: 2023945903

ISBN: 978-1-956578-42-3

For my father,
Olympic Athletic Trainer,
baseball coach, mentor, and hero.
He gave me his name and his shoes,
which were too big to fill.

Author's Note

As a kid I grew up in the locker room at Pittsburg State University, then called Kansas State College. My father was the athletic trainer, and I was continually at his side. I even had my own plastic doctor's bag with a roll of tape in it. The young men who played the game were my heroes. They treated me like a mascot and a member of the team. I could see no other future than as a "star" football player. Upon entering secondary school, I attempted to play the game with boys who were bigger, smarter, and stronger than I was. We went through a lot together both on and off the field. I'd like to mention all their names, but I won't for fear of leaving someone like me, a bench warmer, off the list. One evening, I was reminiscing with teammate Steve Eichhorn about the bull in the ring drill. Steve saw the negative direction of my comments and said something like: Yeah, but it taught us how to take a hit. For better or worse, that was true.

Table of Contents

COYOTE LOVE

1

The mercury light by the barn had been dead for years, but I could see a little because Nancy left the car door open. Lyle slid across the seat and tried to get out on her side. She slammed the door shut, and it smashed him on the shin.

"You bitch!"

I winced.

"Serves you right," Nancy said.

A skinny shit like Lyle Cuff doesn't swallow pain well.

He kicked open the door with his good leg and hobbled after her, hopping on one foot. Then skipping. She raced up the steps.

"Don't think you can run from me."

He grabbed for her shoulder, missed, and fell onto the steps. That gave her time to make it through the door. I was glad I'd forgotten to lock it. I heard her throw her purse down on the table. Bowls and glasses rattled and crashed to the floor. Lyle rolled in the grass holding his leg. Nancy switched on the kitchen light, and it flooded over Lyle's crumpled body. He gimped on one leg up the stairs.

Nancy had swung the door shut so hard that the chain lock caught in the jamb. She ran water in the sink, too drunk to know the door hadn't latched.

Lyle shoved himself across the floor, grabbed her shoulder. She screamed and a water glass broke against the refrigerator.

It's tough to fake sleep when your mother is getting beat up. I picked up my BB gun that was leaning against the sill and crept down the stairs in my stocking feet.

Just as I shoved open the kitchen door, Lyle slapped her. Walloped her a mean one across the face. Her lip split, all blood and popcorn flesh. She fell across a stepstool, overturned it, and crashed against the cereal cabinet. Lyle stood over her, clenching and unclenching his fists. His chest was heaving like Gator's did when running sprints. Gator usually looked more like an action hero though—the senior we all admired, doing what made him great. Lyle, standing over my mom, looked more like the villain.

I pumped the BB gun. He swung around to face me.

"Get out," I said.

Lyle held up the palm of his hand like he was going to give me a speeding ticket. "Stay out of this, numb nuts."

"Get out." I raised the barrel into his face. Weasel eyes. Pointed chin. Helmeted in mouse-colored hair.

He knotted his brow. The BB gun, a 30-30 look-a-like, just like the western saddle gun, was loaded but wouldn't do much more than sting up a welt. I hoped that Lyle thought it was the real thing. He screwed his face tighter into a knot. I liked the feeling of power the fake rifle gave me, even if only temporary. To pull this off I'd have to stay in the dark of the living room so that cowboy Lyle couldn't see beyond his drunk blur.

His eyes riveted on mine. I shivered inside. Guns were not new to Lyle, more a way of life. He'd held plenty. Maybe aimed one at someone like me. Only difference being that his were real. If I flinched, Lyle would knock me snotless, maybe worse.

"Get out." I motioned towards the door.

Lyle glanced once at Nancy on the floor. She was frozen, her hand to her busted lip, eyes like a cat's. He sauntered over to where I stood in the shadows of the living room and pointed a finger at my nose, his gold ring glinting with kitchen light. I backed up a step, keeping the Daisy pointed at the spot where his eyes burned.

"That's a BB gun, shithead. You can't chase me out with a damn toy."

I considered my options. All slim. "A BB can still mess up your eye." I poked the barrel at the bridge of his nose.

Lyle jerked. "You're one dumb bastard." He was right. But I didn't say a word.

He raised his finger in my face again and wagged it like a cigar before kicking the screen door open. Merle dashed under his leg. Lyle swung his boot. Missed. He clunked down the steps, stumbling against the geranium.

"Bullshit." He threw the pot into the driveway. The car door squeaked, popped when he pulled it open. I followed Lyle to the door. He wasn't driving his El Camino, but a rusted '57 Chevy, the same one he'd kept in our barn last winter. A POS project just like Lyle.

Nancy and I waited until we heard Merle meowing, rolling in the dirt and pot shards.

"Lyle's an asshole," Nancy whispered, half into my ear and half into my shoulder.

I almost laughed in her face. It was either that or cry. Like, right lady, tell me something about anatomy I don't know, but I let it slide.

She was broken-vase sorry, sorry for the broken glass, her ceramic life of booze and men. I get nervous when she starts to break down, so I just patted her back.

"Everything's going to be fine, Nancy." And I gave her a little squeeze to show how much I meant it.

"Lyle Cuff's a jerk," she said, wiping her nose on the wash rag I'd given her. "You stay far away from him."

Lyle Cuff hadn't always been an asshole. Once upon a time, he'd been only half an asshole. He took me fishing when I was in eighth grade. Taught me how to cast. One Christmas he gave me a Shakespeare rod. I found out later that he'd stolen it out of the back of a pickup truck. A few months later he took it out of the closet for a fishing trip and I never saw it again. So yeah, he had a good side on a sliding scale that went mostly down.

I tried to ignore the thought of Lyle coming after me. I knew he could kick my ass. I played it down, hoping that Nancy would agree, and I could believe my own delusion.

"Lyle's drunk. Stoned crazy drunk. He'll sober in the morning."

Nancy held my shirt by the collar like she was trying to wring sweat from it. She shook me, her face scrunched red from tears and alcohol.

"You listen to me, Danny. Lyle's no good. Don't matter if he's drunk or sober. You stay clear."

These last words came out slowly like they were being dredged out of a river. And then she sunk to that terrible self-pity place where you hate yourself a lot, I mean a whole lot, but not enough to change. I knew the pattern, the same sad familiar. I could deal with tears, self-pity, whiskey, even a crazed Lyle Cuff, better than a mom who promised motherhood but couldn't deliver.

When I got her lying down in bed, I turned out the light and left her to cry herself to sleep. She wouldn't cry long. The whiskey weighed heavy, her eyelids sagged, wet newspapers wrinkled with bad headlines.

Back in my bedroom, I shoved my flea market recliner up to the window. Tomato Road disappeared at the rise before Cliggett City. Two o'clock in the morning, a pair of headlights crept slow and steady out of town, the arc of the lights searched across the fields. A coyote trotted between the house and the barn, his small shadow blending into larger shadows. The entire night balanced on the tip of his nose. He sniffed, dropped to his belly, tensed to run.

2

Merle likes eggs—cooked, raw, still inside the chicken. I like eggs fried, sunny side up to be exact. Nancy wouldn't be up for hours, and then she wouldn't eat. But fried eggs just didn't feel right, sitting there in the grease with their yellow eyes staring at me, so I stirred them with a fork into a scrambled mess.

I've seen the way men look at Nancy when she's shooting pool at Elsie's Good Luck, but when she walked into the kitchen that morning, she looked like a hairball on a piece of toast. Her lip was swollen the size of a plum, and there was blood on her chin. I don't think she'd bothered to look in the mirror. But then, she probably didn't want to. Can't blame her. Her hair was matted and snarled and the circles below her eyes had turned to purple half-moons. She looked twice her age. She leaned into the kitchen and wobbled, one hand on the door, the other attempting to cover her lip.

She focused her eyes. "Don't be going out today before we talk."

I looked up from the skillet. "About what?"

"About Lyle last night. I don't want you running into him for a while."

I suppose that blew the hell out of my black-out theory. She was a totally conscious drunk last night. I turned back to my cooking, not knowing what to say, not really caring to say anything.

She went on. "Danny, you don't own a gun."

I shrugged.

"You think I didn't know that was your BB gun? That was a stupid thing to do."

"Want some eggs?" I turned around and raised the skillet of scrambled eggs into her face. She paled, then greened, and for a moment I thought she was going to lose it right into my pan. If she had, I would have chucked it out the door, pan and eggs. Coyotes don't care. She covered her mouth and backed up a few steps.

"Gross, get that out of my face."

I held it there, half smiling. Pissed that she'd come into the kitchen to chew me out. That she was hungover. That she dated a jerk like Lyle Cuff.

"You eat something, Nancy Prego." I almost felt the same sorry for her that I did when I was a little kid. Almost.

"Don't go till we talk. Hear me?" With that she backed out of the kitchen and teetered back into her bedroom. "Bring me some Advil."

I had to hunt for the Advil. They weren't where they were supposed to be. But then again, nothing was where it was supposed to be. I dug around in both the bathroom and the kitchen. Finally, I had to walk out to the barn and look in the car. I found three in the glove compartment. They weren't in a bottle, just floating there among the road maps and dead flashlight batteries. Aspirins, not Advil. I looked closely before I saw the Bayer logo. I didn't want her flipping out on some party narcotic.

Back in her room, she was crashed on her bed. Pillow over her head to keep out the light. I thumbed a smudge off the dirty aspirins and gave them to her with a glass of water. She looked pitiful, frail, run-down. I tried not to look at her at all. I don't like seeing her all broken down before she's old enough to be broken down.

"Thank you," she croaked. "Would you close the blinds?" She swallowed all three aspirins, gulped the water without moving her head.

I closed the blinds, shut the one curtain.

"Danny?"

I paused at the doorway, like there was something important hanging out there above the faded quilt and the tissue-cluttered end table. Sometimes you wait for answers, even when you don't know the questions.

"We'll talk later. OK?"

Merle leapt on the foot of her bed, arched his back, and began to lick egg off his paws.

"Sure, Nancy." I closed the door between us.

3

By evening, Nancy still hadn't moved much. She had walked through the kitchen a couple of times as she went out to the dryer, digging for jeans. She never said anything about how clean I'd scrubbed the kitchen. She said she had the flu. No hangover had ever done this to her. I knew better, but I didn't argue. Around seven she decided to get dressed and drive into town for cigarettes and a Diet Coke. Sick or not, she wasn't going to do without nicotine. We still hadn't talked.

After Nancy drove off. I sat on the roof outside my window until the sun disappeared behind a bank of clouds. Tomato Road seemed to empty right into it like a drainpipe. The bean fields caught the last rays of the weekend. Slowly, they disappeared in the darkness.

Somewhere I read that of all the wild animals alive today, one species has actually increased in population due to man's chopping back the wilderness—the coyote.

> *Three coyotes trotted*
> *out of the darkness, leapt*
> *the fence and followed*
> *Tomato Road. I smacked*

*my hands together. One
looked my way, the others
jogged on, knowing better
than to stop for any man.*

4

Later that night, my clock radio reported a truck hijacking, the third in as many months. The driver, although unhurt, had been locked in the trailer, free to pound on the metal walls. The truck carried liquor. Sheriff Douglas said on camera that the investigation of this hijacking and the others was current, so he couldn't speak on whether they were connected. I thought to myself, like hell you can't. Of course they were connected.

Nancy Prego was supposed to be on the night shift at Monroe Chicken, "The Chicken Factory," a rendering plant, source of summer jobs for teenagers like me, and the only real money producer in the whole of "Pullet County." If the chickens ever decided not to come to Monroe to die, then the entire economy would be in the soup.

I didn't feel sorry for Nancy. History taught me that she wouldn't have the night-chicken-shift for long. Gizzards and hearts were as temporary as the "uncles" she brought home with her. At least, that's what she told me when I was a kid. I had a lot of uncles. Some stayed a night or two, others for weeks.

One thing I like about Tomato Road is the hill. The pavement curves over this rise in the fields. Just enough so that when you look between the trees you see the lights of Cliggett City. Well, most of Cliggett City. Old town is farther east beyond the tracks. Except for my house, the poor, mostly Mexicans, live on the other side of the railroad tracks. A cliché even in 1979. Anyhow, the valley glows with lightbulbs. That's Cliggett City. A dump by day, but by night, well, someplace else.

My house sat in darkness, plunged in a complete blackout like before an air raid. Nancy wasn't home. Nothing new. Before this job, she stayed out late so that she could find herself the right man. Hunting for him like fishing. Some of the guys at the chicken factory are out late, setting limb lines with bait from chicken parts they steal, carried in old bread and sandwich bags. She plays catch and release. The problem is that carp don't stay fresh long in the heat of Nancy Prego.

Once, I brought a catfish
home from the river. I didn't
want to throw him back,
too beautiful, so I let him
swim circles in a five-gallon bucket.
When I came back an hour later,
he'd floated belly up, as dead
as if I'd gutted him. That's the way
Nancy's relationships run.
Circles in a bucket. Before long,
they float up, dead and stinking.

5

On school days I caught the bus at the end of our driveway. I rode it to Grover Elementary and then walked the remaining two blocks to Cliggett City High. There was something disgraceful about riding the bus at my age. Some of the special ed kids were on my bus. They got off at Grover at the Special Ed Co-op. One little guy with thick glasses and a briefcase liked to sit by me. His mom would put him on the bus each morning and then be waiting for him on the ride home. In August she'd walked onto the bus and put him in his seat. I was glad she didn't kiss him on the forehead or give him a spit bath.

Franky Weathers. I tried to call him Frank, not Franky. Just like a regular guy. But no matter how I tried it kept coming out as Franky. You could say we were friends. It wasn't long before he started to sit next to me. He wouldn't talk much and what he did say was garbled like he was always sucking on a jaw breaker, but he listened well. I could tell him anything, and he sat there like a shrink. He repeated phrases, the key points in our conversation. I wondered how much he understood, face screwed in concentration, head cocked.

At first Mrs. Weathers was suspicious like I was giving Franky trouble, like I was going to swipe his lunch money or give him the royal flush in the boy's toilet. Maybe I was just paranoid. One day she didn't come all the way onto the bus. She told Franky to go on in and sit by Danny Prego. That's what she said, Danny Prego. It floored me. I thought I was invisible on the bus. Invisible most places. Franky's mother was about as removed from my world as the President of the United States.

When I walked by Franky's house tonight, the lights were on, and I could see him jumping around the living room. He was playing with his dog. Some kind of high energy terrier.

The television, a blue light.
The street and the house lights
momentarily equal,
passing in their change
from day to night.

I stopped for a minute and watched. Window peeked. I guess that means I'm crazy. It was not like I put my face to the glass or anything, not usually, but I do look when I'm on the street. I imagine what's going on. Like, with Franky, I wished I were him. You know, simple, like a TV and a dog were all that mattered. Enough. I reminded myself that when I got home, I had to find Merle his catnip toy.

GREEN CHICKENS

6

Wimps walk. That's a stupid thing to say but that's what I was feeling. I tried to walk like I didn't care if I owned a car or not. I wanted the world to think that I chose who I was. When I got to First Street, I turned down a ride from a couple of sophomore bench warmers. I guess I'd become a snob freeloader. By 6th Street, Gator pulled up to the curb.

"Hey wild man," he said. "Get in."

I didn't have to be asked twice. Beth and her boyfriend, Ronald McDonald, no shit, like the Hamburger Clown, had just left the stoplight, and I wanted her to see me in Gator's GTO. Not that it mattered to her whether I was in a GTO or a Volkswagen, what mattered was that she saw me with Gator. Maybe I'd rate a second glance.

"Where you heading?" Gator Man asked.

"Just around."

"No car, huh?"

"Nancy's got it." Half a lie. She did have the car and the dead battery.

Gator dropped it into first and we headed out into traffic. He didn't seem to mind that I was with him. He stopped for me and that was blowing my mind. During the first days of the season, he hadn't even known my name. Now, we were driving down Main together. Over the past few weeks a few of the seniors had started talking to me in the hall. The benefits of being naked together each afternoon in a locker room. Ammonia stink and football.

"Want a beer?" Gator dug two cans of Busch from a paper sack on the floorboards.

"Sure."

Gator took three long gulps. Sighed. "Coldest beer in town. Elsie's."

"Yeah." I took a sip.

He stopped at the first light. I could see Beth and the Clown across the intersection. Her head bobbing, blonde hair moving as she made a point. I knew the gesture, had memorized it. She talked with her whole body. What could she be talking about with that guy? The light turned green. As we passed, Ronnie and Gator waved. Not a big wave, but an easy hand on the steering wheel wave. Beth blew a bubble. Didn't notice us.

I was disappointed. Took a drink.

Gator tossed his empty from the window and was fumbling in the paper bag.

He handed me a second beer and I put it between my legs. I took a second drink out of the first one and felt the carbonation un-corroding my battery terminals. "Sure is cold."

Stupid. Saying something dumb as *sure is cold*. Simple simple simple.

Gator turned up the radio. He said something about driving over to Chicopee to screw with the Hawk fans at the bowling alley, and that he was supposed to meet up with Angel and the Murphy brothers. Chicopee was only fifteen miles away. Cliggett City people visited whenever they needed to see a cow or a hog or roll a bowling ball. I'd made the trip enough, but never with seniors.

I was with the Alligator himself. Long-haired. Thick-shouldered. Cannons for arms. Heading to Chicopee, not a country road or gravel turn-around, but a bowling alley parking lot in a rival town with cops and cowboy-thugs.

"Good idea," I said, beer dribbling down my chin.

Gator rolled down the window and gave a rebel yell to the moon.

We met Angel Chavez at the Dairy Mary. Gator got out of the car and motioned for me to follow. Chavez seemed surprised to see me, but he didn't say anything. Grinned. We gathered in the back of the Murphy brothers' truck. Most people thought they were twins. But they weren't. One had been held back in grade school. No IQ maybe. I didn't know. The Murph brothers were cocky. The carhop asked if we wanted something to drink. Gator said that we needed five frosted mugs, hold the root beer.

The brothers drove a dented Ford pickup, one that after years of farm work had been parked behind the barn for the field mice. We sat in the back on the sidewalls, scuffing paint flakes with our feet. Everybody had a sack of Busch. I held a bag for the empties. Angel said he didn't want any evidence rolling around for the cops. Brian Murphy gave me another coldest beer in town. Pulled it from his brother's sack. Nice guy. When the cops drove through the parking lot, we held the cans between our feet and sat, arms crossed on our thighs. One waved at Angel.

Angel said, "Hello, Deputy Barnett."

The brothers preferred country music. Gator climbed in the cab and switched the station to Rock & Roll. The Stones.

Brad Murphy said, "That was George Jones."

Gator said, "Yeah. I know."

"They're not even Americans," Brian said.

"Neither is Angel," Gator said.

We laughed. Angel worked his pop tab free from his can.

"Only Indians are American," he said.

We laughed.

"I'm serious."

The brothers shut up. Gator crunched his beer can, then flattened it under his boot. "Well, I'm as much Indian as any of you."

"Bullshit," the brothers said.

"One left," Brad said.

Brian rattled his sack without looking inside. "Only empties." He pushed it to my feet. "You're in charge, Scud Boy."

I tossed the sack into the empty pickup bed next to us, ignoring the Scud Boy. A scud is a low life. Trash. A bottom feeder. I didn't like the name, but I decided to live with it for a while.

"Let's run out to Willy's," Gator said. "I'm a long way from done."

Angel slapped his hands on his knees. We turned to him as our leader. He was our quarterback after all. "I think we need some chickens first."

That dumbfounded me. *Chickens*, I thought, *like fried chickens?*

The Murphy brothers lit up simultaneously. "We've still got the green."

"Yeah." Gator said, clapping his big bear paws together. "Perfect."

The brothers jumped out of the pickup bed and opened the doors. Gator eased himself over the tailgate, springs releasing. Angel drop kicked an empty can and it soared into the street.

In an instant I was the only one left in the truck bed.

"You coming, Scud Boy?" Brian asked.

I loved fried chicken. I could eat. I had a five-dollar bill. "Sure," I said.

"Danny can ride with us," Angel said. He motioned to the back seat of Gator's car.

Back in the Goat with the bad boys.

Saturday night was looking up.

We drove past the turnoff to Willy's Truck Stop, the only place I knew where we could get fried chicken any time of night. They fried it in back during the day and kept a mountain of it under warming lights for the drunks and all-night truckers.

"Wasn't that the road?" I asked.

Gator smiled, stepping on the gas pedal, the *Welcome to Cliggett City—Chicken Capital of Kansas* sign flying behind us. The Murphy brothers were right on our tail, weaving in and out of our taillights.

"Take the back way," Angel said. Then he turned to me and gave me a mischievous smile.

"Back way is the only way," Gator laughed.

I laughed like I knew what he meant.

I knew where we were. That's a start. I rode it all summer, either on my bike or with one of the Mexicans from the trailer park off Tomato Road.

"This is the road to Monroe's," I said.

Angel flicked his long hair out of his eyes.

"They serve fried chicken?" I asked.

Gator burst into laughter. Angel followed, shaking his head. "No man, not fried. But they have chickens."

"How many do we need?" Gator asked.

Angel took a moment as if counting pieces of white meat, dark meat, combo plates. "About twenty chickens should do it."

"Twenty!" I said. "I've only got five bucks."

Laughter erupted from the front seat again. I was immediately sorry I'd said anything.

"Pull over." Angel pointed to the parking lot fence behind Monroe's.

The nightshift was in full swing. Lights shone through a row of high windows. The long doors pulled open for night air. Two employees smoked at the entrance. The loading docks were quiet. One truck sat in the shadows, running lights aglow.

7

ngel and the brothers scrambled over the back fence and disappeared into the shadows beyond the truck. Gator and I parked behind Utility Shed 4. We crept up to the fence and waited. "The dock door is always open," Gator said. "Not much changes in chicken world."

"You guys rustled chickens before?" I asked.

"If I tell you, I got to kill you," he said.

"That's a yes."

"Maybe. But never just for fun."

I looked up quizzically.

"Christmas suppers. People Angel knows."

"What's that mean?"

Gator shrugged. "Just saying. Angel knows people who've got nothing. At least on Christmas they get a chicken or two. His old man told us how to do it."

"Mr. Chavez!"

"No. Coach Amber. Who do you think?"

Angel's dad ran the day shift on the docks at Monroe's for as long as anyone could remember. He was a small, wiry guy with a buzz haircut, tattoos on his arms. I'd seen him at games and here at the factory. He was an older version of his son. Dark hair. Dark eyes. Athletic build. Angel wore his hair to his shoulders. His old man shaved his close like a Marine. Both wore western boots. Angel had the height on his dad by several inches. Both commanded respect without being jerks.

"Don't say I told you."

I shook my head. "Monroe's has plenty of chickens."

"Old man Chavez said we were serving the Blessed Virgin of the Chicken Factory. Monroe's has more chickens than Jesus."

Gator unwrapped a ten-cent cigar and stuck it in his mouth. He kept it unlit. "Here they come."

Three shadows hurried across the lot, lugging a wooden chicken crate between them.

"Just got one," Gator observed.

As planned, I climbed on Gator's shoulders, and we stood up at the fence. The brothers were laughing.

> *chickens wobbled with each step*
> *the brothers took. strangely quiet,*
> *a few clucks, nothing more.*
> *as if they knew dying*
> *as well as living*
> *but suspected nothing*
> *more*
> *than the next minute*

"Lean over the fence," Gator ordered.

I did. The brothers lifted and Angel shoved from behind. I grabbed the crate by the side bars and hauled it back over the fence. The smell of chicken shit enveloped me. I yanked so hard that the wooden crate smacked me in the nose. Eye to eye with the saddest looking hen I'd ever seen. Gator grabbed the bottom of the crate and we stepped backwards into the shadows. Angel and the Murphs scrambled over the fence. Pointed toe boots were perfect for climbing chain link.

We slid the crate into the back of the Murphys' pickup.

We slapped a round of high fives, then Angel said, "Let's go. Keep your lights out till we hit the main road."

8

At the Y intersection, the Murphys went right towards Chicopee while Gator turned left back to the truck stop. I threw in my five-dollar bill, and we bought more Busch. We met up with the brothers an hour later behind Chicopee High School in the brick alley between the school building and the football field. In the shadows Gator lit his cigar. The chewed, wet end looked more like a turd than a butt. Brian and Brad jumped out first and raised the crate out of the pickup bed. We joined them under a sign that said *Hawk Power*. The chickens and the brothers dripped with green food coloring. Chicopee Hawk colors.

"Damn," Gator said. "You guys look as bad as the chickens."

I had to agree. Their hands and arms up to the elbow were stained green. Jeans splattered. Boots streaked.

"The spray bottle exploded," Brian explained.

"Screw you," Brad interrupted. "You sprayed that shit right into the damn wind."

Gator handed them a couple of beers. "Don't let anyone in town see you till you get cleaned up."

Angel dug through the toolbox until he found a pry bar and a small sledge. "Keep your eye on the road."

The Murphs drove their truck to the edge of the alley and parked next to an evergreen. I walked behind the welcome sign so I could see the other intersection. Gator took the sledge and pry bar away from Angel and wedged it between the doorjamb and the door. He swung the hammer against the end of the bar three times in quick succession. The door to the Hawks' locker room popped open. The Murphys twittered. The chickens twittered. Angel tipped the crate up on its edge, spilling green chickens into the green locker room. They cackled and strutted among the jockstraps and chalkboards and dripping shower heads. They wobbled, confused in the darkness.

"Green's a good color for chickens," Angel said before slamming the door shut.

"A weekend to shit without interruption."

"Pluck it," Gator said.

9

A challenge. I imagined something like the old black and white movie that Nancy watched on AMC. James Dean. *Rebel Without a Cause*. You know, where the main hoodlum drives his car over a cliff. It's all terrible and pathetic because you know nobody wants him to die, but he does anyway; his coat caught on the doorknob or something and he can't jump out. And then the car goes over a cliff. Anyhow, when we got to the parking lot of the Bowlarama, it was ass-full of bowlers, old guys with gray hair, beer guts, names stitched across their tight shirts. Saturday was league night.

The Murphs ran their truck through the carwash twice to get the green out of the bed. They sprayed each other, boots, legs, arms. Still faintly spaceman green, they gave up. They hid the truck behind the city park. We squeezed into Gator's backseat. Angel riding shotgun, me with the dripping twins. It was almost romantic.

"Best car in town," Brian said.

"Damn right," Gator said.

"I wish my grandma would buy me one for Christmas," Brad said. "All we get is soap on a rope."

So that's how he affords it, I thought. Gator's dad was a plumber. He made good money, but still, a GTO is top shelf. A grandma gift.

"Up yours! She loaned me the money."

"Sure, she did," Brian said. "And you'll pay her back like never."

Gator stomped on the gas, and we bounced against the roll and pleating of the back seat. "Keep your asses on that blanket. That leather's worth more than your farm."

"Hey!" they said. "That's low. Maybe we saved a chicken for the car. It'll stink like the Hawk locker room."

We laughed. Gator sucked a glow onto his cigar.

10

I knew my place, and up until tonight, it had been on a bus seat next to a Down's kid named Franky Weathers. Each time a new phase of the night started, I was still included. Gator lugged the car around the parking lot in low gear, no easy task in a maze of parked cars. One thing about bowlers, they don't know how to park. Cars were wedged like gutter balls.

Gator drove slow. It's cool to drive slow when you've got a badass car. Keep it in first, goose the gas once in a while. When he hit the pedal, our heads flipped back like bobble heads, then snapped forward to a beer. Then we drank. With each Busch, I liked drinking more. Gator crept over speed bumps, one wheel at a time.

"Mount Fuji bumps," Angel said. "Snowcapped until spring."

Dale Reynolds, the team's center, waited on the far edge of the parking lot, back where the asphalt turned to gravel for overflow nights. Beyond that there was just some cut grass and then bean fields and the rest of Kansas. The Bowlarama was on the edge of town, at the end of the known world. Stuck in the middle of the back seat, I couldn't see, but it looked like Dale had Chavez's girlfriend with him. I'd only seen her once before. But they said she was out of high school. I didn't know if "out of high school" meant graduated, expelled, or quit. I didn't care. In fact, I was beginning to care less and less about more and more.

Dale Reynolds was a stud, not as big as Gator, but All-League, maybe All-State. He was also smarter than Gator when it came to schoolwork. Low bar. I knew he was a straight-A student, classes like chemistry and physics. His dad was a lawyer. From what I heard, his old man was strict as hell and a friend of Lyle Cuff. Go figure. He had money, but he forced Dale to work the hayfields every summer and at the Foodtown in winter to pay for his truck. To pay for his everything. Even rent.

Dale sat in a rusted '57 Chevy Bel Air. Rita opened the passenger door. The clunk it made was the same clunk that Lyle Cuff's had made the night before. I hated thinking about Lyle Cuff.

11

ator wasn't going to do the roof thing until he saw the '57, then he whooped. "Nothing can hurt that car," he said.

I had to agree.

Gator parked the Goat and we all climbed out into the Indian summer air. I followed the crowd until I was standing next to the girls. Shoulder to shoulder with Rita. She was beautiful. No doubt about it. She had dark eyes like obsidian, like pools of deep water. Not cute-sexy like Beth. But young woman sexy. World knowing sexy. She smiled at me like a little brother, and that made me happy and sad at the same time.

One of the girls was Rita's cousin, Candy. She was my age, a junior. She smiled. I smiled as dumb as a plant. Probably a rubber tree. OK, maybe she was pretty, I guess, but not knock out pretty like her cousin. She had bumps for breasts. Gator's were bigger, but I thought I shouldn't tell him that. Dale had his arm around her.

Gator stepped up on the rear bumper and began to climb up on the roof when Angel stopped him. "Let me go first," he said. "Then we all go." That must have made sense, because Gator jumped down without an argument and Angel climbed up on the trunk.

"I want to do this freeform."

Gator said we should rig some rope through the windows and string it up over the top like reins, but Angel refused.

"No way," he said. "Cliggett City Blue Devils have been challenged."

"Who's going to see?" I asked. I hadn't seen anybody but bowlers and more bowlers.

Rita said, "That's right, Angel. There's nobody here except these little bowler men with their blue balls."

We laughed. I pressed my legs together.

Angel balanced himself on the roof. Tonight, Dale drove like Gator's grandmother. Angel bent his legs at the knees, one leg in front of the other. If you'd ever seen surfing, then it might look like that, but to me it just looked like he was standing on a car roof, his balance perfect all through the gravel. But at the first speed bump on the asphalt, he collapsed on the roof. Gator howled. Rita pretended to be worried. But she was laughing.

The roof crunched when Angel fell, but Dale didn't show any concern. He kept driving. Standing, arms out, Angel rode towards the front of the bowling alley, flexed over the next speed bump, and rode it effortlessly. Dale didn't slow, nor did he speed up. I could tell right away that the key was a steady gas pedal. Dale had a steady foot. Dale was a steady guy.

Two bowlers came out of the Bowlarama and stopped short at the awning. Angel turned, dropped his pants, and mooned them. Even from across the lot, we could hear him, "Smile for the camera." The man grabbed his wife's arm and tugged her back towards the door. Dale swung the Chevy in an arc around the row of parked cars. They hurried back inside.

"That was boring," Angel said as they rolled in beside the GTO.

Dale stomped on the brake and Angel lunged forward. To keep from losing his footing he had to jump crazily onto the hood. Then onto the grass in front of the bumper. When he hit, he tucked his head and somersaulted like a gymnast. He stopped upside down with his head poking up between his legs.

<h1 style="text-align:center">12</h1>

"All of us," Angel said, his head still wedged between his legs. "Everybody on the roof. Rita drives."

"Let's break the record," Gator said.

Rita untangled her boyfriend, and we dug the last of the beers out of the sacks. There weren't enough to go around so we had to share. We stood in a semi-circle and passed the beer. Like a brotherhood. More civilized. Sharing beer is a sign of maturity. Zeppelin streamed from Gator's windows. "Stairway." Dale lit a joint. Sang the lyrics. I was happy.

Angel arranged us on the roof, explained the importance of flexing over the bumps. It took a few minutes to get organized, because the bigger guys had to stand in the center and anchor the rest of us on. Dale was still singing. There wasn't enough room, so it was Gator and Dale in the center with the alien-green Murphy brothers to Dale's left and right in back. Angel and I were in the front on either side of Gator. Three in front, three in back. We locked arms. Rita drove. She was right below me. She patted me on the shoe. A cigarette was between her fingers. It looked like a Salem.

Rita drove faster than Dale. She bumped right into the parking lot without hesitation. "Watch the road," Angel said. "Keep your eyes on what's coming."

"I can't see shit," Dale said.

The Murphy brothers were laughing again, giggling like little kids.

We hit the asphalt and Dale lurched. We leaned back into him, and he steadied. *Cool*, I thought. *Teamwork.*

"Tell me what's coming," he said.

"Something's coming," Gator said.

13

Angel called out instructions like in a huddle, play by play, bump by bump. Giving us all the info on the pavement ahead. Speed bump, and we all bent our knees. Ready. Now. And it would be under us, and we floated over like it was nothing. Rita kept a steady foot on the pedal. The Chevy growled like a fat dog.

"Everybody turn and wave. We moon 'em second time around." We followed Chavez's orders, turning, and waving at the front door. The bowling league jammed under the awning watching the Blue Devils from Cliggett City. We circled the parking lot once without mishap and I thought we were going to stop, but Rita didn't even slow. Not even when Candy jumped out and got into Gator's Goat.

"What the hell?" he said.

"You left your keys," Rita laughed.

"Hang on, dickheads," Chavez snapped and we glued our attention on the parking lot. Two cars had just driven in, and they were full of cowboy hats and Hawk letter jackets. I could see the green and gold gleam in the flood lights. A third car followed, and I was surprised to see it belonged to Ronald McDonald. Beth was with him. One more chance. I wanted her to see me dancing in senior world with the wild crazies, Gator, Angel, the brothers. I wanted her to see the beautiful-eyed Rita and wonder if I was a part of her world.

The next car that pulled in had cherries revolving in bright red circles.

"Jump!" Rita yelled out the window. She stomped on the gas. Gravel spun into the lights of the GTO.

We fell. But Rita didn't stop. The Chevy accelerated, fish-tailing in a wide arc out onto County Road. Dale pitched backwards and rolled head over heels across the trunk. He spread eagled in the parking lot. The Murphy brothers fared no better. One of them slid off the side of the car, the inertia of Rita's turn spinning him out into the night. The other kicked a hole through a cloud and disappeared off the edge of the roof. I fell off the side of the car and was kept from becoming a smear on the asphalt by pure Gator-aide. He had a hold of my belt. Angel gripped the rain gutter.

I hung over the side of the car eye to eye with Rita. She turned the wheel so hard that her elbow banged me in the nose.

"Sorry," she said, like she just stepped on my foot at a homecoming dance.

Hanging upside down, unable to right myself, the parking lot and then the street racing under us. In a blur, we passed the carload of letter jackets, their gold chevrons glistening like fillings in a mouth. Then the Hamburger Man, his jaw dropped, mouth in a big O, Beth beside him, her blonde hair tied back behind her head. I waved. She waved. Danny, I thought she said. Then I saw the Sheriff, not the Deputy, but the genuine voter-elected Sheriff himself. Lyle Cuff stood beside him.

I groaned as the Chevy lurched out onto the county road, scratched rubber once and slid into third gear towards the darkness ahead.

Gator hauled me to the roof once we'd straightened out. "Hang on," he yelled, like I needed reminded. We grabbed the narrow gutter, bellies down, faces into the wind. Behind us I could hear the low throb of the GTO gaining on us. Far behind it, a siren.

"Pluck it," Gator said.

"If she gets caught . . . in this car . . . with us . . . it's jail," Angel said.

What about us? I thought. The wind whipping, the roadside flying.

Gator spread his arms wide. One across my back, the other across Angel's. The pressure was reassuring. But an illusion.

"She . . . won't . . . get caught," Gator said, the rushing night air swallowing his words as quickly as they were spoken.

"Danny," Angel leaned my way. "Tell Rita . . . take the next . . . dirt . . ."

"Road" was lost somewhere between the wind and the throbbing motor, but I knew what he wanted. As I leaned over the roof, Gator's grip tightened. I thought I was being mashed into rusty metal.

Even hanging off the Chevy's roof upside down in a high-speed chase, she was beautiful. The whole crazy night sparkled in her earrings.

She was driving with her hands at ten and two. Very proper. *Nice*, I thought. Feeling oddly safer.

"Next dirt road."

She nodded. Didn't bother to turn her head from the road, but I did catch a little gleam in her eye.

Her lips parted. She turned her head and smiled.

"You're cute," she said.

I stared dumbly at the speedometer, glowing green in the shadow of the dash. Gator winched me back to the roof.

"Really fast," I said. "Maybe eighty." The speed of the Chevy was only part of the reason why my heart was pounding. "Cute" raced through my head faster than the wind.

Rita slowed, turned into a cloud of dust, the Chevy spun right, careened left, jerked right, then straightened, plowed on into the tunnel of the headlights. Tree limbs whipped my legs, and I could see hedge apples on the road. One caught the front tire,

popped
   like a bullet
     into sadness

14

The GTO had disappeared, probably straight on towards Cliggett City, or it had been stopped by the Sheriff. Behind us a cloud of dust billowed. Dark limbs hung above the road like fingers that could snatch us off the Chevy's roof.

"Witches Hollow," he said.

I'd heard of it. Ghosts. Chainsaws. Hanging tree limbs. Haunted make-out spot. Where girls could pretend to be scared and boys could fake being fearless.

Angel beat on the roof with his fist. "Turn off the lights."

"She can't hear you," I yelled. But she must have been thinking the same thing. The road plunged into darkness.

"Slow down!" I smacked the windshield with my palm. She did. A little. The road was barely visible. What moonlight there was had been sucked up by the clouds, only a dim gray road appeared. She drove fast, too fast to turn, too fast to brake. The road S-curved by the creek before the iron bridge.

The Chevy skipped the turn, flew through a barbed wire fence and into a bean field. The field had been let go. Bean whips snapped against the fenders as we bounced across the furrows,

42

dust and bean plants flipped over the hood into our faces, then behind us into the night sky. I rode a tornado.

Suddenly, the front end dropped. Gator was airborne. Weird, like I had time to speak to him. I could have said, *Good-bye Gatorman. Thanks for the ride.* Air birth. Air death. I hung in flight, my body between the clouds and the beans. I was going to meet Jesus. I said nothing. Sorry for the stolen chickens.

Oddly, I wondered if death would be accompanied by "Stairway to Heaven."

My body exploded in a cloud of dust, arms, legs, and ragged plants. My face hit next, fire to my forehead. Something big and ugly thudded my upper thigh. A tree stump, a gnome, a fleeing coyote. It's funny what you think about when you're almost dead, somersaulting through a Kansas field.

I lay in silence and took count of my body parts. The thought of paralysis leapt at me. Could they get me on the school bus in a wheelchair? Maybe I'd have to be taught at home. Nancy would have to slip me in and out of bed and bring me my Cap'n Crunch each morning. Right! Fat chance. Merle the Cat could wipe my butt.

Was I still cute?

It was quiet. Nothing. No car. No wind. No voices.

A dark hulk limped across the furrows.

"Gator?"

He stopped and turned towards me. "Come on," he said. Then he turned and resumed walking. The car was nowhere in sight.

15

Gray smoke rose between the trees. I could make out the path of the Chevy through the beans. Gator was in the middle of it. An airplane had crash landed, cutting a long, clean swath. I wobbled after him, swinging my leg behind me, cupping my nose.

Steam hissed from the radiator, thick with the smell of anti-freeze. My first thought was that the car was going to blow up, but Gator didn't seem concerned. He short-stepped down the gulley where the car had plunged. The headlights were back on. They were glowing under the water like the city pool's at night. Instead of blue and friendly, the water was brown, a murky turd-chocolate.

Gator slid down the mud into the water. He opened the car door and a wave of dark water rolled in. I skidded on my butt into the creek.

"Help me," he said.

I climbed back up the embankment, kicking toe holds with my tennis shoes. Gator eased Rita out of the car into the water.

"Take his hand," he said. And Rita looked up at me with those dreamy eyes, now hurt-filled, a gunshot doe. I knew I was falling in love, just as assuredly as Chevys don't float. I held her arm.

She slipped. I helped her up the mud embankment like I was escorting the most precious commodity in life. A real girl on my arm. I tripped twice.

Rita didn't remember much. She said, "It's all a blur of beans and darkness."

No kidding. That's exactly how she said it. The front-end bouncing, headlights off, beans torn from their roots, flipping like snakes across the hood, smacking the open window with their rasping pods.

My face had begun to ache, and I was afraid to touch my nose. When I did, my hand came down covered with blood. I used the tail of my flannel shirt to sponge my face clean. It burned like I'd taken a potato peeler from my chin to my hairline. Nose-dived into a bean row, not into the waiting arms of Jesus. Gator looked fine, his surfer hair messed up as usual.

16

We found Angel in the hedgerow, cradling his arm, and leaning with his back against a tree. His silence said something was wrong.

I hurried over to him, Gator and Rita followed more slowly.

"You okay?" I asked.

His eyes widened like he were coming out of a dream. "Not really," he answered. "Effed up my arm."

"Let me see."

Angel shook his head. "It's broke."

"What's broke?" Gator was standing over us.

"His arm."

"Let me see."

Chavez didn't move.

"Let me see your arm," Gator insisted.

He uncradled his arm and lifted it with his good hand.

"Where's it hurt?"

Angel nodded towards his forearm. Gator squatted down in front of him and began to test his arm, slowly from the elbow down. I guess he'd seen Coach do it before. About two inches above the wrist, Angel winced and drew it back. Gator let go.

"I don't feel shit. Maybe it's just a sprain."

Rita sat beside Angel and stroked his hair. "I'm sorry, baby. I'm sorry." She had begun crying, large fat tears rolled down her face like rain drops. I noticed that her blouse was open and that her tears were running down behind the cotton. I wanted to put my arms around her and tell her it was OK. That it was nobody's fault. Accidents happened. Later, when my heart had cooled, I realized that yeah, a lot of what happened was her fault. There was no reason for a freaked out highspeed chase once we got to the dirt road. She was just roaring on adrenaline.

Angel ran his hand through her hair. "Nobody's fault. You couldn't get caught."

I didn't see why. I had more to lose against Lyle Cuff for standing on his car roof than any of them did.

We met Dale and the others while walking on the dirt road. The Sheriff had passed him and gone on after us. Dale had turned back to Chicopee to get the Murphs' truck. Then he'd driven back out looking for us.

"Sheriff lost us when you shut off the lights," Angel said.

"I about lost you," Rita said, taking Angel's good arm in hers.

"There's something I need to tell you about the car," Dale said as we settled into the backseat.

"What did you do to my car?" Gator exclaimed in alarm, leaning forward in his seat to examine the dash.

"Your car's fine. Be glad I drove it, dog."

"Damn straight," Gator said.

"The other car. The Chevy."

"It doesn't float," Gator said. "Your old man is going be pissed."

"I borrowed it without asking."

Gator snorted. "Dale Reynolds stole a car. No way."

Dale drove. Eyes ahead. "I borrowed it."

"It's Lyle's car," I said.

Angel leaned forward from the backseat. "Tell us," he said.

A blue jay pecked
my window. He bounced
along the windowsill,
tapping his beak against the glass.
An oddly familiar bird had invaded.
Peck hop peck hop.
He squawked, fluttered, puffed.
That was Sunday.

17

Monday morning rain. A drizzle coming off the eaves. Tapping the window like fingers. If it weren't football season, I'd have stayed in bed. Merle had curled next to my head. He put out heat like a ten-pound furnace.

After I showered, I dragged out an old trunk of my dad's from the closet. It held what Nancy couldn't look at or throw away. Things that hung in this limbo of mothballs. Things that didn't mean anything to anybody except me. Like a well-worn pair of western boots. They were good, real leather, oiled. Tony Lamas. I held the leather loops at the top and shoved my foot. A snug fit. I did the same to the other foot, smoothed my garage sale Levi's down over the uppers and stood up. I flexed my toes. The boots had this warm, I-know-you feel to them, like I'd been wearing them all my life. We belonged together.

I can tell a lot about a person by the shoes they wear. There's this one kid at school who wears Vietnam jungle boots, canvas and leather, laced up high and tight like an introvert. One senior girl wears heels. No kidding. All day clicking the tile floors of Cliggett City High School in heels. *Click click click.* She prefers clicking to speaking. She dates a college guy. My old friends from freshman and sophomore classes were diverse. Sneakers, sandals, penny loafers. No kidding. I liked them, but we weren't tight. Loose tongues. Slippery soles. Broken laces.

It was good, standing on the back porch, the gray rain falling, knowing that I was wearing my dad's boots. Boots that he'd taken the time to polish and oil. The leather grain was still a part of him, and except for when I was young, this was the closest I'd been to him. I thought about it every time I looked at my feet.

18

On the bus I felt taller. More confident. I sat down in my usual seat. Even the bus driver said hello. It was like he was seeing something different in me. I leaned back in my seat and stuck my legs out into the aisle. Not rude or anything, just visible. When the little kids got on down the route, I moved my feet so they wouldn't trip.

Franky's mother poked her head into the door long enough to see me. She smiled. I gave her a nod. Franky sat down beside me. He talked about *Star Wars*. He stared at the scrape that ran the length of my face.

"Ouch," he said.

I planned to get off at the elementary school as usual. I still didn't want to be seen riding the bus. Angel or Gator could ride a bus full of bookworms with briefcases and penny loafers, and before the end of the day, everyone would be fighting to ride the same bus.

But things didn't work right. When the bus driver pulled up at Grover Elementary, there was a scrum of ninth graders waiting to get on. The bus drops them off last. These guys didn't usually ride with us. Usually, they took Bus 8. I knew they meant trouble for Franky. Junior high kids are second only to convicts or mad dogs when it comes to being cruel to people weaker than them. They move in packs and when they see someone like Franky, well, they eat him.

Two of them were my size. Probably freshmen. They were smoking when the bus stopped, and they flipped their butts at the tires. Tough guys. They shoved their way up the stairs. The bus driver, Mr. Simms, tightened his fingers on the steering wheel, checked his rearview mirror. He's not the best for keeping law and order. One of them saw Franky. He nudged his friend with his elbow.

I knew the game. They would make Franky move to the back of the bus after they teased him a while. It had happened before. The best way to get Franky riled was to mess with his glasses. Last spring, maybe the same clowns had rubbed spit on his lenses. Franky started screaming. The bus driver, Leo something, hadn't seen what happened, but he did hear Franky go crazy, so he kicked him off the bus at the high school bus stop. Franky's mom went ape shit at a school board meeting. The bus driver was fired.

Anyhow, I saw it coming and so did Franky. He put his hands on his glasses. His body tensed. I climbed back up the steps and pointed my finger at the two largest piranhas. They laughed like I was nothing, but I kept the finger in the air, an inch from the leader's nose. It was the finger wag I'd learned from Lyle Cuff, king of assholes. I'd made up my mind to trade punches. And they knew it.

Shit kickers. The bus got quiet. Old Mr. Simms stepped into the aisle. The two ring leaders shoved a kid in front of them and walked to the back of the bus.

I sat in my old seat next to Franky. I rode along with him to the Co-op.

19

Two years ago, Coach Amber brought a few of the freshman football players up to practice with the varsity. He must have had a shortage of tackling dummies. The team was short of juniors and seniors. Short of winning, too. Freshmen owned the basement. The two floors above were for high school classes. A small school thing. Coach started sophomores. Personally, I was thrilled to make it onto the high school team. I even enjoyed practice. Less time at home. Less time alone with just Merle.

I had no problem with the radio station or the music. I'm a rock and roller like the rest of the team, but it was the radio that got me in trouble that Friday. Control of the only radio is a power thing, and who controls everything on a football team? The starters. I really had no trouble with that either, the starters make the team. They earned the right to control our lives for a few hours a week. My deal was that I was bored and pissed off with the world. It just so happened that I was lying on the floor with a couple of other special team bums right where the first extension cord connected with the second extension cord.

I unplugged the cord at the center court line, and the gym dove into silence.

This big guy, a sophomore called Gator, groaned to his feet and ambled off towards the locker room to plug the cord back in. It was reasonable to think that it had been disconnected in the office. I let him reach the door and then I plugged the two ends of the cords back together. As expected, when the power died somebody had turned up the volume. Deep Purple. Loud like a battle. Gator shrugged and walked back towards his spot on the floor. Just as he was ready to sit down, I unplugged the cords again. Dead music. Smoke on the water. Gator sighed and headed back the way he'd come. Sort of like ping pong. Gator was the ping and I held the pong. This time I didn't let him get as far as before. I snapped the cords back together. The team roared and Gator turned around red faced and steaming.

"The sucker's going crazy!" he stammered.

More laughter. Gator sizzled.

He almost made it back to the offensive huddle when I stopped the music again. That was one time too much, because he turned and faced the center court. He'd begun to suspect a plot. That's where I screwed up. I stood with both ends of the extension cord in my hands and began to plug and unplug the prongs as fast as I could. "Smoke on the Water," here one second, gone the next.

"Get the scud!" Gator yelled, and then he was after me, followed by the rest of the team.

I slipped and someone grabbed my ankle. I went down hard on the wood floor, smothered in a dog pile below the climbing ropes. My nose bent to touch my eyebrows. I blew boogers on my forehead. My lips were smashed like I was kissing a baseball bat. Somebody grabbed the back of my pants and jerked. My underwear disappeared up my butt. I choked on the elastic. I heard them rip. They tugged again, and this time, my balls followed my Fruit of the Looms into my butt crack.

From under the pile, I caught a glimpse of Angel Chavez's face. He was sitting against the wall, smiling at me, like he admired what I'd done to Gator. Angel was our quarterback.

The climbing ropes were as thick as pythons. Hard to tie around a pair of skinny ankles. They were wrapped tightly several times and cinched with a knot. I struggled to get free, but every time I moved, my underwear choked me. I could taste cotton.

Struggle was hopeless. I was pinned to the floor, my legs wrapped with itchy hemp. I had to rest just to breathe.

Gator said, "Haul the scud up." The ropes dug into my ankles. I swung upside down.

"Let him go. Let him go," he said again, and I felt the dog pile disassemble itself. Fresh air swept over me. I sucked in cool air, rocking free of the floor, my fingertips just barely dragging against the polished hardwood. The Murphy brothers held the rope.

"Stop. Don't kill him," Angel said. A small wave of relief drained down my spine. He was still in charge. Quarterbacks are known for their brains.

I was hanging in mid-air. I was doing all I could to keep from getting pissed off. When swinging upside down above the gym floor in front of your teammates, it's best to pretend like you're cool with it. So that's the attitude I copped. Like OK, it's all good. But what I couldn't stop was the real embarrassment. A steamy redness flushed my cheeks, roared in my ears like a toilet flushing. I pretended like I wasn't feeling anything. But I was certain that everyone on the team could see me reddening up, swinging there in the middle of the gym with my jockey shorts stuck up my butt.

Upstairs the rest of the school was going about the business of high school. Typewriters were clacking. Pencils were scratching out essays. A bandsaw was screaming in the shop. Frogs were getting pithed by over eager lab assistants, but I was far removed from that. I had left my body long enough to watch the scud kid pendulum upside down in the gymnasium. I carved a corny smile out of the pumpkin of my head and stuck it on my face like a jack-o-lantern. The coins in my pocket slipped out and clattered on the floor.

"Coach coming!" A voice rang out. It only took seconds for the team to be back on the floor, spread out, talking quietly like it was an everyday occurrence to have a freshman swinging by his ankles in the middle of the gym. "Can't Get No Satisfaction" poured out of the radio.

Coach Amber eased through the doorway from the lockers in his usual slow and deliberate manner. As head coach, Amber kept his cool both on and off the field. There wasn't much diplomacy with Coach. He'd praise you when you did well and kick you in the ass when you didn't. The guys admired his iciness and tried not to get frost-bit.

The radio was clicked off. Only the slight squeak of the ropes as I swung a few inches to the right and then a few inches to the left disturbed the hush. I planted my fingertips to slow my spin.

Coach had walked in with his back turned to me. His head was shining through his Marine haircut. The muscles of his back bulged, his neck a weightlifter's V, his legs bowed like an orangutan's.

He scratched his nose, droning on about the necessity of concentration on a game day. He was making some point about how psyched up our opponents were at this very minute. Maybe the game meant more to them than to us.

The team was exploding. They could see me and Coach couldn't. They weren't making a sound, but they were going crazy inside. Gator's fat face was so red that I thought that he was related to a tomato. Angel buried his chin into his arm. The Murphy brothers had large clear tears running down their cheeks. I knew what was next. Coach was going to say something about the team that had the "want-to" was the team that won. Without the "want-to," men were nothing. A typical coach line taught at coaching school.

Just before he made his big point, he paused. Probably for dramatic effect. He moved just enough to catch me out of the corner of his eye. He turned. We squared off. Coach Amber. Bulging neck muscles. Simian legs. Blue and white whistle lariat.

And upside down me. Special team's sling shot. Roped and ragged. Coach almost smiled, but he swallowed it down like it were liver and onions.

"Mr. Prego," he said, "if you tell me who hung you up there, I'll cut you down."

The Murphy brothers untied me while Coach looked on. "So, tell me!"

The team grew silent.

"Coach," I said, "I really don't know."

"Bullshit," he said.

"No really. I fell asleep during a Bee Gees song and when I woke, I was all tied up."

Coach turned to face the team. No one but Angel met his eyes. "Tell me, Mr. Chavez," he said.

Angel examined his cowboy boots. "Coach, it's like the kid said, the Bee Gees came on and I zoned out."

Gator grinned.

Coach nailed us with one of his long stares. "Team dinner is being served in the cafeteria. No more goddamn horseplay."

As the team walked out of the gym, I waited until they had filed ahead of me, and then I ducked into the john and pried my underwear out of my asshole. I felt better immediately. I could breathe.

"You did good, Danny."

Angel Chavez came out of the far stall. He was zipping up his pants.

"About what?" I answered in my best who-gives-a-damn voice.

"You know. You could have had the team running sprints until midnight. Monday would have been hell. Sprints kill Gator."

He gave me a thumbs up and stepped out of the pisser before I had a chance to answer. I felt dumb for not answering with something cool, but inside I was swelling with confusion. I trotted down the hall towards a plate of watery pasta, thinking about bread and butter and being one of the team. My step was uncertain, but my underwear was in its place.

I told Franky my story. I know he liked it because afterwards he leaned his head on my shoulder and handed me a Tootsie Roll Pop. Orange. His favorite. The problem was that our situations were so different. Franky did nothing to deserve what the bus bullies gave him. They would never be his teammates, much less his friends. I know bullies. The king of bullies lives part time in my house. Besides, Gator would have strung up anyone who messed with his music. He was free of prejudice.

20

I'm one of those guys who goes to school without books, paper, pencils, and sometimes, even lunch. I didn't believe in homework. I guess you could say it was against my religion. I believe in lunch. A lot of the guys carry brown paper bags, because the cafeteria could kill even a cockroach on bad days. But there wasn't much at home this morning. Besides, I liked for people to think that I bought my lunch across the street at the Snack Shack. I could usually scrounge up a couple of bucks on most days. Sometimes hunger isn't as bad as humiliation.

Usually, I carry a library book. Lately, my thing was poetry. Not roses-are-red-mush, but real poems from Ginsberg, Bukowski, Snyder. Miss Finch, my sophomore English teacher, had ignored the syllabus and brought us beatniks. Coffee shops. Finger snapping. The class had been slow to catch on. But she gave a lot of As and Bs, so she won us over. She'd started us out with this one little poem about a red wheelbarrow. I didn't understand it, but I couldn't get it out of my head. We studied song lyrics; Morrison, Plant, Henley. I haven't been the same since. I missed Miss Finch. She treated us like we were real people. She wanted us to think and to write what came into our heads. I've been writing poems and stories ever since. They're private. I keep them in a notebook that fits in my jacket pocket. I write in pencil, so I can erase. Miss Finch said one day I'll be confident enough to use ink. That cracked me up. I wore old hiking boots to class that I'd found at Goodwill. They were seldom laced. Miss Finch let some students eat lunch in her room. Mostly her honors class. It was an open door for anyone who appreciated a good pencil and a blank piece of paper. That's what she said anyway. I suppose Kansas was too flat to keep her from rolling away. The school board hired the English teacher I've got now. He's good at giving assignments like answering the questions at the end of the story. We skip poems mostly.

Teachers left me alone if I was reading. I remained invisible. I was a poem-reading ghost. In fact, until today I'd never wanted to be noticed by teachers or coaches or principals. Today, I had Dad's boots. I was taller.

Cliggett City High School is in one of those ancient 1930s style buildings in the middle of a residential part of town. The steps are worn, grooved in the center by years of use. I liked the way my heels clicked as I stepped firmly in the center of each groove. One of many who had buffed the shine into the marble.

I heard a familiar engine throb pull up the drive. It was Gator. He was slouched over the wheel like he didn't care that the first bell was ready to ring. I waved, but he didn't seem to notice. My arm hung there in the air for a moment, then I stuffed it in my pocket.

As soon as I walked into biology, I could tell that today wasn't what it was supposed to be. The lab tables were set up for a test. Mr. Sanders, a dick, was famous for his high-pressure exams. The kind where we moved from station to station throughout the room. At each station we had two minutes to answer a couple of questions, or to identify some part of a flower or a dissected frog butt. He kept the class under constant stress, counting out the time. Forty-five seconds left, thirty seconds left, fifteen seconds left, time's up, move to the next station.

I could hold my own on these tests because I paid attention to Beth's notes. Plus I didn't really care how I did, so I wasn't nervous. Once, this kid named Galen Green dropped onto the floor in a dead faint. Mr. Sanders had to call the school nurse. By the time they got Galen cleaned up off the floor the time schedule was all messed up, and Sanders cancelled the test. No one complained, but what blew my mind was that the very next day, he had an entirely new exam ready for us. Man, that guy was a machine. Beth said he was completely type A. I didn't know what that meant, but I pretended like I did.

I'd counted on spending the class period near Beth. Playing it up as friend to the cool seniors was stolen by an exam. I hadn't studied. But then I never studied so that wasn't new. I wasn't in the mood for a test. I sat down on the little metal stool just inside the door of the lab and sucked in my breath. I felt robbed. The class was putting their books and notebooks in the lab drawers. I slipped a pencil out of Mary Thompson's notebook when she wasn't looking.

The room was hot from the row of steam heaters along the wall by the windows. Too hot because of the cold snap. A heavy smell of formaldehyde hung in the air. The biology room always smelled of formaldehyde. It turned my stomach, rolled it over on itself like I was going to puke. That's why I sat down. Biology class on an empty stomach isn't easy. Finally, I saw Beth sitting beside Galen Green. She was giving his notebook a quick cram. They were talking, nodding their heads like they knew what was on the test. For a moment, I wished I was a good student, like Galen, so that Beth would be talking to me.

Beth looked up from her notebook. I was watching how her lips formed the word *photosynthesis*. I couldn't hear her, but I knew that was the word. She was sexy when she used big words. Once I thought that oral sex must be all about talking it up. In Beth's case using big words. I know better now. Sometimes I think I could sit all day and just watch her read a dictionary. Her eyes caught mine, and for just a second, she smiled. Then she went back to her notes. I was a little deflated. I thought about going over to see her, but Sanders had started reading off our names. We each were given a number, and that number showed us at which lab station we would begin. I was so far away from Beth that I may as well have been floating outside the window. I glanced around to see the order we'd be following, and nowhere could I see where our paths would cross. Nowhere. I mean it would take an out of the body experience to get near her. And if I was out of my body when I got near hers, then what good would it do me?

I stood at station six. I couldn't see the questions because they were inside a manila folder, but in front of me was a microscope slide. It held something like a chloroplast or plant spit. I didn't really care. I was angry and my head was starting to hurt. Ten minutes inside this building and my whole day had changed. Sanders said start. I looked around to make sure that no one was watching. No one was. The class was zoned in on their questions. I scribbled something on my answer sheet, slipped the microscope slide out of the little holder and scraped the plant spit off on the bottom of the stool. Then I put the blank slide back and was ready for the next move.

Station seven had a coleus plant in a beaker of colored water. I didn't even bother to read the question. I knew it had something to do with vascular systems. I took the dyed plant out of the colored water and crunched it up in my pocket. Just when the lab assistant walked out of my peripheral vision, I dropped Mary Thompson's pencil in the food coloring.

Station eight was another microscope. I wrote *marijuana* on the slide with a felt tip that was left at station seven. The more I screwed things up the better I was starting to feel. Already the kid on station seven was losing it. Twice now he'd taken off his glasses and rubbed that little bone between his eyes. He tapped his pencil eraser and wrote something down on his paper. It killed me that he'd even try to fake it. A pencil in food coloring? Lead poisoning?

Around station ten, I heard somebody start to cry. I looked over my shoulder and it was Mary Thompson, the girl I'd swiped the pencil from. She was Miss Special. She carried this large canvas bag with a happy face on it. Whenever she set it on the floor, books slid out of the top like fruit in a cornucopia. I hated happy faces. As she cried, sniffling really, I could see that she'd reached her limit of failure. She wasn't used to coming up blank. I remember thinking—*how's it feel baby*—smiling to myself. By the next station she let out a whimper like a wounded animal. I felt sorry for her. So much failure . . . so little time.

The kid at eight threw down his pencil. I was feeling smug. I mean, all these nerds thought there was a problem that could be solved. It must have been a lot like having the phone ring and not being able to get the person on the other line to hear you no matter how hard you yelled . . . *hello!* . . . *hello!* . . . *hello*! The misery was starting to crack me up.

Mr. Sanders tried to calm her. It was pathetic.

She said, "I'm trying so hard . . . *sob* . . . and I can't find . . . *sob* . . . anything . . . *sob*."

Sanders patted her shoulder. "Now Mary," he said, "it must just be out of focus." He bent down into the eyepiece, frowned, adjusted the focus nob. Frowned again. And then examined the *marijuana* slide. He slammed the slide down on the table so hard that it shattered. I guessed he had cut his hand, but he hadn't.

Then he moved the next kid over and looked at the pencil/ coleus. He lifted it from the dye, examined it, and slipped it coolly back in the colored water. I'd have felt more comfortable if he'd thrown it against the window. Because now I knew he was beginning to think. A cold light flickered across his face.

"Put your pencils down," he told the class. And we did. Some who'd already hit the sabotaged section did so with relief, while others parked their pencils. Sanders worked his way from station to station. A little voice in my head said I was dead. I moved out of the way to let him look at my diagram of tree rings. I'd just added another arrow with the inscription *Dark Sarcasm.* And then to the next station where everything was in its place. Sanders put down his clipboard and stopwatch.

"Class, return to your own lab tables. This test has been temporarily postponed." Then he turned to me. "Danny Prego, follow me."

My knees wobbled as I followed Sanders out the door. The class watched open-eyed. Some were eager, witnesses at a public hanging. I could have sold popcorn. For Beth, I tried to pull off the smug tough guy routine, but she wasn't smiling. Her cheeks were red and her eyes were watery like she was embarrassed for me. That bothered me somehow. I don't know what I expected, maybe that she'd cheer me on like Rita would have. She didn't.

Sanders marched until we reached the office. He left me at the little bench by the secretary's desk and stepped into the principal's office. The world dimmed. My headache banged a drum solo. I crossed my legs and squeaked my thumb against the calf hide uppers of my dad's boot. Good leather.

21

I passed Angel on the way into the locker room. He waved his new cast, his face clouded like the sky outside. I knew immediately Coach had chewed his ass out. I wanted the story. I wanted to know what had happened in Amber's office, but there weren't any answers. He gave me that little cast wave and then was gone down the hallway towards the shops. Amber wasn't happy. You lose your starting quarterback, and it changes the world. He went into his office and closed the door. I could see him frowning as he stared at his *Coach of the Year* paperweight. He put one of the seniors in charge and the class did calisthenics all hour. No kidding. Push-ups, deep knee bends, sit-ups, running in place. On and on. At the shower bell I got motioned into his office. As soon as I closed the door, I knew he'd heard about the biology test. His face was red and knotted. There was this one deep furrow which ran just above his eyebrows where his forehead slipped down to his nose. When he was mad, it deepened. The madder he was, the deeper the furrow. When I sat in the wobbly wooden chair by the door, the furrow above his nose was so deep that it looked like the Grand Canyon. I could see pack mules leading tourists to the river.

"You see this." Coach pushed an official looking pink memo to the edge of his desk. I thought it was going to slide to the floor and disappear out of sight, but it hung there on the wood grain. Even gravity was against me.

"Yes, sir. It's from the office."

"Yes, it is. Mr. Prego. From the office. You know what it says?"

I could guess.

"I think so," I said.

"I'll bet you do." He slid the paper back across the desk and quickly scanned it. "Says here, you're a discipline problem. That you've been kicked out of class. A science class. Is that right?"

"Yes, sir."

"Can you explain yourself?"

My mind was blank. Nothing new. Three fourths of this season was over, and I still hadn't ever been able to carry on more than a yes sir, no sir, conversation with him. He didn't give me time to answer.

"Forget it. I don't want your answer."

My mouth closed like a trunk lid.

"I'll give you your answer. My football players are not screw-ups. They don't get kicked out of class. Got it?"

I did. Knew it all along. "Yes," I said.

"Do you want to play football, Prego?"

"Yes," I said.

Coach dropped my pink slip on his desk. He folded his hands in front of him.

"This morning I received a phone call from the Sheriff. Chicopee High School was broken into and vandalized. Someone released farm animals in the football locker room. You know anything about it"

"Farm animals?"

"Chickens are farm animals. Wouldn't you agree?" Coach said.

"I suppose."

"You suppose?"

"I mean, yes sir."

"They covered the locker room, the coach's office, and the equipment room with chicken shit."

My first reaction—laughter. Yeah, we got'em.

But Amber wasn't smiling. "You know anything about it?"

My vision blurred. "No, sir."

Amber's eyes drilled into my brain. "What did you say?"

"No sir!" I repeated.

Amber tapped his fingers on his desk. He waited for me to add something to my statement. "Several Cliggett City letter jackets were seen in a Chicopee parking lot."

"I don't have a letter jacket."

Coach ignored my last comment. "A vintage car was stolen. A high-speed chase followed."

"A vintage what?" I stammered.

"A car. An automobile. You know anything about it?"

"No sir," I said.

Coach leaned across the desk. "You were seen."

"Me?"

"Someone gave the Sheriff your name as one of the Cliggett City students in the parking lot."

"No sir."

"No sir, what?"

I was momentarily confused. "I don't have a letter jacket."

"Forget the letter jacket."

"OK."

"Someone fitting your description was in the parking lot. Stole a car. And led the Sheriff in a chase across the county." Coach turned his fake paperweight ninety degrees to the right.

"No sir."

"No sir, what?"

"It wasn't me."

"The Sheriff wants names. I want names. I don't want my team ruined by a bad apple. Are you the bad apple?" He tapped the paperweight with his finger.

"No sir," I said.

"Then tell me who is, and we forget about this." He held the pink paper between the fingers on his other hand. "If not, we'll see how much you want to stay on the team."

The sky, fat with rain, hung above
the practice field, all mist, all worry.
The boys with glasses
wiped their lenses with their fingers.
Still, they couldn't see.
The temperature dropped. Clouds
searched the earth with long fingers.

22

Practice is bad on Mondays, especially after we lose a Friday game. Tonight, Coach worked us hard, bone-cracking hard as we went over Friday's screw-ups. Then part way through practice, he huddled us up and said the past was behind us, and now, it was time to look towards this Friday with Lincoln. If we lost to Lincoln, then we could forget the playoffs. Everybody wanted the playoffs. It was a team goal. It meant everyone on the traveling team lettered. That meant me. I wanted to wear the jacket, like I was someone.

Coach Amber ran us. I hate sprints. More than almost anything. But tonight, I thought they meant that Coach had forgotten the Bull in the Ring and the names he wanted to squeeze out of me. I ran with abandon. Hoping that I'd been spared. Hoping with each dash that I was closer to the locker room, but I should have known better. When we were doubled over for air, gasping as we lined up for the next wave of sprints, Amber blew his whistle. The evening was so gloomy that Coach had turned on the stadium lights. Circles of mist hung around each light like halos. Angel stood beside the chain link fence. He gave me the thumbs up. I swallowed, choking on phlegm.

"Circle up!" Coach yelled. Suddenly everyone was standing around me. It was weird. But they all knew. I mean, I never heard anyone say, we're going to play this game, and Danny Prego, you're it. They knew.

They knew the Bull in the Ring. I was to go one-on-one with each member of the squad. It began when a teammate's number was called and ended when a whistle blew. Then the next guy's number was called. The problem with being the bull was that you weren't allowed to even breathe much less rest between one-on-ones. After a few hits, you don't see too well and can't tell where the next guy is coming from. You're surrounded. If you get knocked down, you're dogged until you get up. Then you get knocked down again. The only way out of the ring is to knock heads with everyone, wait for the coach to end it, or quit the team.

I had to suck it up. Standing in the November mist, the water beading on my facemask, I felt more alone than I had for a long time, more than when I squared off against Lyle.

Amber blew the whistle three short blasts. I loosened myself at the knees, legs bent, arms dangling at my side, rocking like a linebacker.

"Seventy-two," he bellowed.

Troy Welch flew down on me in a full sprint, his cleats throwing divots of mud. I ducked and lowered my shoulder. We slammed together, my pads burying themselves in his gut. I thought I'd absorbed most of the impact when suddenly he caught me with a double forearm in the chest, lifting me off my feet and into the air. I landed on my ass. The team *ooooohed* in unison. I shook my head and jumped to my feet, thinking the worst was over. Welch rode bulls at the rodeo. My sternum ached.

"Sixty-four!" Amber hollered again. Joe Taylor came after me. He was fast. I was fast, and we just sort of smacked helmets. Not a good way to hit. Too upright. But I wasn't thinking of form or style, just survival. We slid off each other and I heard the next number. I chop stepped, turned hard to the right, and met Sam

Butler with my shoulder. He was a sophomore, smaller than me, and he landed on his butt. I had enough air to laugh.

Two of the assistant coaches jumped in. One yelled, "Forty-six." A second later the other yelled, "Twenty-nine! Eighty-four." They came at me so fast that I'd no more responded to one than another wrung me up, a pinball bashed by flippers. My head throbbed. My lungs burned. My body wasn't mine, gasping like a dying dog. Footsteps pounded.

"Fifty-one!" I heard Amber shout. A radar bleeped in my head. Mertz. I squinted, but between the peppering rain and the blur of dizziness, I couldn't see him. I straightened. He hit me directly from behind. Whiplash in auto accidents. Wow. My head jerked backwards like it was ripped off my spine. My feet gave out from under me and the next thing I knew I was face down in the dirt. Flipped. My facemask dug, burrowed through the rubbery grass, spraying my nose and mouth with mud. I could taste the practice field between my teeth. My teammates reeled as I tried to stand. Then I caught another blow on the right and it toppled me over. The bean field scab ripped off. Blood trickled down my face and into my mouth. I couldn't feel it, but I could taste it. At the time I didn't know what had happened. I was so stunned from Mertz that I didn't hear the next number. Bucky Thompson, the safety, plowed me under again. I recognized him because he always wore a black sock and a white sock.

I rolled upright, legs like spaghetti. Strings of mud and grass were hanging from my facemask. I gagged on a wad of snot and hawked it towards the circle. Some of it hung from the bars of the facemask, arched towards the blur of practice jerseys.

That's when Amber yelled two numbers at once. Double teamed in the ring. The Murphy brothers flew at me like angels of death. I didn't expect Dale or Gator or the brothers to cut me any slack. No one did at practice, except maybe in sprints, but never in contact. It was one of those understandings we had. You screw up, you hurt. Well, the only thing that kept me from getting clotheslined was that when I heard them running at me from opposite directions, I body-blocked at the ankles the one that was the closest. It was a good move. He tripped and crashed into his brother. I heard their helmets crunch. Coach didn't blow the whistle and they kept bulldogging me as I tried to stand. Each time I started to my feet I got knocked down, again. "Stay down," Brian said in my ear. "Almost over."

Finally, in frustration, I took a last strength leap and tumbled towards the edge of the circle. One of the brothers dove for me but was only able to catch my ankle. It twisted under his weight, and if I hadn't lost my shoe, I think I would have sprained or broken my ankle. I hopped on one foot towards the jerseys that stood before me.

I wobbled to gain my balance, struggling to stand. I wasn't going to lie down. Travis Miller, a shit-eating second string nose guard, stepped out of the circle and fore-armed my helmet. I dropped.

It's expected to get thumped in the ring. Travis Miller popped me with his bear paw. It was ugly. Coach hadn't called his number. He caught me off guard and decked me with a cheap shot. That was it. I lugged myself out of the mud and screamed something Biblical into the stadium lights. I ripped off my helmet and went after him, swinging it like a club. Amber started blowing his whistle as Miller began dancing.

Miller made one mistake. And that was side-stepping towards Gator's side of the circle. Very few people liked Travis Miller. The cat calls were in my favor. But I was out of gas. One shoe was off, and my sock was a muddy mess. Scab blood stained my jersey. Miller backed out of the circle. Gator stepped in front of him and smacked him with a dirty forearm to the chest. Miller exploded. I could smell the onions on his breath from lunch. He collapsed in the mud. I started to swing my helmet down on his facemask, but the Murph brothers caught me, unclenched my fingers from the helmet. I dropped to my ass, cross-legged.

Brad tapped my shoulder pads. "No killing in football practice," he said.

The locker room cleared slowly after practice. I was so tired that I couldn't take off my shoulder pads. Gator lifted them off over my head, laughed, and punched me playfully in the shoulder. Even that hurt. But I didn't let on. The other guys were avoiding me. I suppose to let the misery bleed out of my wounds. I didn't care. Not feeling much like a hero, I found a hot shower and stood under it, numb, blank. If I didn't move, nothing hurt. When I tried to soap myself, I found out that I couldn't lift my arms above my shoulders.

I lathered my hands and lowered my head far enough to soap the mud from my face. Then I rested. The hot water steaming around me. Gator and Miller had been called into the coach's office after practice. I could see them getting one of those sportsmanship lectures. Coach would ask if they wanted to go one-on-one tomorrow to solve their differences. He didn't allow fighting, but a one-on-one grudge match was different, built character he said. Miller was a chicken shit. No way in hell he wanted to meet up with Gator again. Coach let him off the hook with a warning, and a couple of extra sprints tomorrow night. He refused to punish violent enthusiasm.

I lowered my head and ran my soapy fingers through my hair. Two huge clumps of mud came out in my hands. I couldn't figure how mud would get up inside my helmet. But it did. I ignored the pain and rubbed my hair vigorously under the showerhead until my hair squeaked. When I walked out of the shower a few minutes later, everyone was gone, except for a couple of managers in the equipment room. There was still a light in Coach Amber's office. The coaches took turns staying late. I guess tonight was his night.

Locker rooms are lonely places when empty. The managers talked and a shower dripped, but other than that the place was quiet as a tomb. I fumbled with my pants. My left foot kept choosing the right leg hole. The boots were the hardest. They were tight. I pulled hard on the leather loops. I grunted, shoved my foot down. Nothing happened. I sat there a minute, breathing. Dave Bryant, the head manager, pushed while I pulled. They slid on.

"Your feet are swollen," he said.

I tossed my towel into the laundry bin, thanked Dave, and stepped outside.

HAIL MARY

23

I knew better than to shoplift at the Easy Shop. There's only one guy watching, but he can see everything. He's like omniscient. Trained by God or the FBI. Whenever a high school kid got busted for shoplifting in Cliggett City, it's because they tried to rip off cigarettes or gum or beer from the Easy Shop. I had a better plan.

A block from the Easy Shop was Cramer's gas station, one of the few remaining stations in the world that still had a bottled Coke machine. A relic. Anyhow, they kept all the returnable bottles in a shed where they dumped the discarded tires. I kicked open the door and picked up a case of bottles. I didn't want to walk in with a complete case. I emptied them in a cardboard box from the dumpster. I added a couple so the number would seem random, like from a back porch.

I liked to think of everything when planning a heist. Not that I did it very often. Just in emergencies like when I was starving. I edged down the alley towards Cramer's when I saw a bicycle leaning against a garage. I took off my jacket and hid it behind a jon boat and balanced the bottles on the handlebars. I rode the bike down the alley into the parking lot. I leaned the bike against the plate glass window so the attendant would see me. He did.

That was the second catch. I had to make sure that I didn't know the guy. If I had, none of this would have worked.

The Easy Shop clerk was an old man with sixties hair and a long gray moustache. If he hadn't been working, he'd have looked like someone Nancy would have dated. But like I said, he was employed. I carried the box of bottles in and laid them on the counter. The clerk didn't say anything. He counted the bottles, put the sack in a wire grocery cart, rang open the register, and laid the money on the counter.

I didn't buy anything immediately. I had to make it look like I wasn't starving, like I'd just cleaned out the back porch and had money to burn. One thing this store had going for it was chicken. Pullet County. They roasted whole chickens on multiple rotating spits. They were cheap, probably picked up wholesale from the chicken factory, like factory seconds.

Crippled. One-legged. I forced myself to look at magazines, and then at chips, and then at candy like I was a dumb kid who couldn't make up his mind. Finally, I carried a magazine up to the counter. Let the guy start to ring up the sale, then I acted like I had changed my mind.

"Give me a chicken, instead."

He pushed his hair back with his hand and extracted one of the chickens from the heated cabinet, slipped it in a white bag, and laid it on the counter. With the money I already had in my pocket, there was just enough for the chicken, a Coke, and a pack of Big Red gum.

I rode the bicycle back down the alley to the garage where I'd found it. And then I started walking home, sticking to the alleys and darker streets whenever I could. If the Cramer's guy got wise, he'd tell the cops to be on the lookout for a kid on a bike. I felt safe. They'd also be looking for somebody without a coat. The cops would think I lived close by, not two miles out on Tomato Road. I liked being smart.

I had one other stop to make before going home. The night was as soupy as when I'd left the locker room. But for some reason it didn't seem so dark or wet with a chicken to eat and Beth Wilkins's house was just a few blocks away. I sat on an oil barrel under a carport and tore the chicken piece by piece. Chicken Capital of Kansas. My body only hurt when I chewed.

Seeing Beth. That's why I bought cinnamon gum.

Every window in Beth's house was lit. Bright, cheery like there was a party going on inside. Mr. Wilkins's Lincoln was sitting in the oval drive. I walked up to the door and started to ring the bell when it suddenly hit me that I didn't have anything to say. I wasn't even chewing my gum, and for all I knew I had chicken grease all over my face. I ducked back into the bushes, stuck a wad of gum in my mouth, then I unbuttoned my pants and tucked in my shirt.

I used the Lincoln's side mirror to wash my face, with fog beads from the rooftop and to run my fingers through my hair like a comb. Most nights I would have just turned and walked away, but tonight felt different. I took a deep breath, stepped back up to the door, and rang the doorbell. My brain rattled with chicken bones.

A woman answered. "May I help you, young man?" she said.

"Can I talk to Beth?" I said.

The woman was Beth's mother. She wasn't as pretty as Beth, but she had Beth's eyes.

"Are you one of Beth's school friends?"

It killed me how when she spoke her head bobbed like Beth's did. She'd probably been cute when she was a kid, just like her daughter.

"We have biology class together." This wasn't a total lie. Once upon a time we did. I was probably kicked out. Her mother didn't need to know the whole story.

"How nice, but Beth's out with Ronnie at the moment. They are at some kind of club meeting. She's due back any time."

"Yeah. We're in some of the same clubs together." That was really a lie. Except for honors English lunch, I'd never belonged to any school activity other than football since the seventh grade's Geography Club. And I only joined that to get out of homeroom one day a week.

"Would you like to wait inside?" The lady opened the door wider like she trusted me, the town pop bottle thief.

"No thanks," I answered, suddenly aware that the chandelier in the front hallway was brighter than any light we had at our house except for the mercury vapor that hung out by the garage. It was brighter than the moon when it worked.

I turned and started down the driveway.

"Did you walk all the way out here?" The lady asked, stepping out from the doorway, the chandelier blossoming in her hair.

Pretending like I didn't hear, I waved.

"Who should I say came by?"

I turned and trotted down the driveway into the street. When I heard her close the door, I stopped and slipped into the bushes. That's when I saw the car swing onto Nottingham. I knew immediately it was the Hamburger Man.

It pulled into the driveway. I moved in a little closer, being sure to stay in the shadows.

"What a jerk," Ronald was saying. "I can't believe he did that."

I froze.

"Well, he did," Beth continued. "Mr. Sanders was going crazy . . ."

I froze more.

Her mother opened the door as Beth was about to turn the knob.

"Oh, hi Mom."

"I heard you coming up the walk. I wasn't eavesdropping."

I *was* eavesdropping, so I slinked behind the Lincoln.

Beth sighed. "Oh, Mom. Like it would matter. We were just talking about this silly boy in my biology class."

As the door closed, the last thing I heard was the Hamburger Man say, "Really immature."

You know how it feels when you step outside on a winter's morning in your underwear. Well, I felt that cold. Iced inside. Iced inside while my face flushed with the heat. I imagined them all standing below the chandelier laughing about the silly boy in biology class, the immature one who skulks in the dark outside of the popular girl's house and rides to school on the bus. Suddenly, I hated them all. Beth, her mother, Ronald, the Lincoln, the chandelier, every house on Nottingham with their fake British names and too-bright lights.

In the shadows of the manicured lawn, I let the air out of Ronald McDonald's back tire. I didn't have my knife, so I had to let the air out slowly by pressing down the pin in the valve stem. It took forever. As I trotted off across the field towards Tomato Road, I was happy that I had not given Beth's mother my name. My finger ached.

I followed the barbed wire
into the old garden site
to get a clear view of the backyard.
Important to know the lay of the land,
whether to climb the elm
and slip in through my window.
One comforting thought that night,
my dad's trunk, sorting the past
calmed me as a cigarette
did smokers.

24

The Sheriff's patrol car and Lyle Cuff's El Camino were nosed in all the way up to the back door. At first, I figured that I'd been turned in for stealing bottles at the service station. The rusted '57 Chevy, as far as I knew, was still stuck grill-deep in a muddy creek off the county road.

There was no sense in climbing through the upstairs window. I wasn't a ninja. They'd hear me. When I stepped on the back porch, the old floor squeaked, and I heard chairs scrape across the linoleum. I almost ran, an instinct I have around cops. I see a uniform and instantly I want to jump a fence. The fields stretched all the way to the truck stop on the highway. If I ran fast, I could disappear in the darkness before I'd gone fifty yards.

But I was just too tired. This was Monday. The same Monday I'd found my dad's old boots. The same Monday I'd ridden to school with Franky. Effed up a biology test. The same Monday I'd faced the coach and then the entire team one-on-one in the ring. Stolen pop bottles. Eaten a chicken. The same Monday I'd been ridiculed by Beth and her clown friend. Now this. The anger that had been brewing since I left Beth's drained out of me like dirty engine oil. It ran down the steps onto the mist dampened sidewalk. I slumped on the steps and probably would have sat there like a Buddha until I fell asleep, but the chain lock slapped against the wooden door and the hinges creaked.

Someone tried to push open the screen, but it stopped when it thudded against my back. I stood up.

"Danny Prego. It's about time you got home. Come inside."

Nancy held the door open. She was being overly formal like she gets when she wants someone to think she's in control. She hadn't called me by my full name since my baptism. She was sober as a stone. That scared me.

When I stepped into the light of the kitchen, it was like stepping into an interrogation room. Lyle was there, of course. His chair was butted over close to Nancy's. Too close. Sheriff Douglas sat at the head of the table. Nancy had cleared away the Cap'n Crunch. His deputy perched on the counter stool next to the sink. A smirk inched across my face like there was nothing unusual about having two gestapo agents sitting at our kitchen table on a Monday evening. But I was nervous, and my smirk turned into a sneer.

"The Sheriff wants to ask you some questions," Nancy said.

"Sit down a minute." The Sheriff motioned for the deputy to get up and he slid off his perch and moved over by the washing machine. It was stacked with magazines and newspapers. I don't think a load of wash had been done in it for years. In fact, I don't think it even worked. Why fix a machine when there's a laundromat? Nancy needed to date a Maytag guy for a while.

I sat down. It was the chair I considered mine anyway.

The Sheriff tapped a pack of Camels on the table in front of him. "Danny, can you tell us your whereabouts last Saturday night?"

"Sure." I answered with a phony confidence. "I went out."

"I need you to be more specific."

"Well, I went walking. I don't have a car. I walked downtown like I usually do."

"You mean, downtown Cliggett City."

"Uh huh." I nodded.

"Did you meet anyone?"

I had to be careful here, because by now, I was sure that Lyle had seen me hanging off the roof of the Chevy at the Bowlarama. How else would he and Douglas know to come to the house?

"Answer the question, son," Douglas said.

"Yeah. I met some guys."

"These guys. Do they have names?"

"They have names," I said. "They gave me a beer." I thought I'd admit to drinking. A thought was crossing my mind that maybe I could play irresponsible. Like I got drunk and didn't remember a thing.

"Danny." Nancy worried her face into a frown. "You don't drink. You hate the smell of it even."

I wondered whose side she was on. But I held to my story. Stupid was the only card I had.

"You drink," I said, anger rising in me like stomach juice.

Nancy frowned and reached into her purse for a cigarette.

"I tried it," I continued.

"Who were these, boys?" The Sheriff asked.

"I'd rather not say."

"Mr. Prego. A young man fitting your description was seen by my Deputy in a truck at the Dairy Mary on North Main. A truck belonging to Lynn Murphy. Lynn Murphy has a couple of boys about your age."

25

The world closed one more notch. I remembered seeing the Deputy roll through the drive-in while we hid our beers in the truck bed. I also remembered how good I felt at the time. Shit changes.

"I don't remember. Sorry."

"Tell me what you do remember."

"Chicken. Someone wanted to eat chicken."

The Sheriff sighed and pushed himself back from the table. "I'm tired of cat and mousing, Lyle."

"What's this all about?" I asked.

"Let me talk to the boy alone, Sheriff," Lyle said.

The last thing I wanted to do in all of North America was talk to Lyle Cuff alone, about anything.

The Sheriff took off his hat and wiped out the brim with his fingertips. "Lyle," he said, "if you think it'll do any good, it's your car."

Douglas motioned with his head to the Deputy, and they walked out the door. The chain lock rattled when they slammed it shut, but at the last moment it slipped in behind the door and swung free of the jamb. For some stupid reason, I was relieved. Like maybe a closed door kept them farther away from me.

85

Through the window, I could see the Sheriff's flashlight gesturing, pointing across the fields.

I faced Lyle. His eyes were black holes. They had a gravity that tried to suck me into them. I shook it off. Just like in any fight, the last thing you want your adversary to see is fear. I turned to anger and thought about that asshole Ronald McDonald. My anger welled up to my chin. My eyes met Lyle's.

"What?" I asked.

"What? You ask what?" Lyle sneered. "You think I didn't see you Saturday night in my car?"

I forced my eyes to stab into his. "What car?"

It was like a knife fight. He stabbed back. "You know, damn well what car. The one you and your hoodlum friends ripped off."

"The Sheriff tell you that I stole your car?"

Lyle narrowed his eyes. "It don't matter what the Sheriff told me. I know that I saw you on top of my car. Some woman was driving."

I had to find a way out of this confrontation. I needed time to think, but I hated Lyle so much that I was allowing myself to get carried away into it.

"Who was the driver?" Lyle cut in.

"I don't know what you're talking about." The thought of getting Rita involved in all this made me cringe. She'd get arrested. That much I knew. Even though none of it was her idea, she was the driver.

"Who were the other guys on the roof?"

Gator, Angel, Murphy Brothers, Dale. Their names clicked through my head like ammunition rounds. My friends. My teammates. The only good night I'd had all school year. Then the memory of Gator stepping out into the circle tonight to club down that idiot Travis Miller popped into my head. Miller had dropped like a sack of rocks. A little smile spread across my face.

"I don't know what you're talking about." I refocused my eyes on Lyle.

Lyle's ears were turning red. Little rivers of steam were rising into the overhead light, the fake copper one Nancy had bought at a garage sale. Lyle twisted his back like he was trying to shrug off a monkey. He hissed through his teeth, shook his finger at me. "Listen, hot shot."

I snapped my teeth like I was trying to bite his finger off. He yanked back his hand.

"You think you're so damn above it, like nobody can touch you. Well, let me just say, your shit stinks like everybody else's." He pronounced it like *ever buddy*. "I've only kept the Sheriff off of you out of respect for your mother."

"The same respect that you smacked her with on Friday," I said.

"Listen, kid," Lyle said. He stopped to swallow. "Your mom and I want something better from all this."

Your mom and I? I didn't like the sound of that.

"We hoped that something could be worked out. That you'd help me arrange to have my automobile returned and those hoodlums apprehended."

Auto mo beel. What a hick.

"That car is worth a lot of money to me."

"That car is a piece of shit," I said.

Lyle's eyes widened. I'd said too much.

"You admit it," he said.

"I admit nothing," I said.

Until this time, Nancy had been sitting in her chair like she was on another planet. She gazed at me through these dull little brown eyes that looked like they were covered with wax paper. She wasn't drunk, but she had probably been popping ludes.

Lyle took a deep breath and patted Nancy's hand. "We'd hoped to start out a little better than this. Without so much trouble from family."

"Family? What's family got to do with your car?"

Lyle put both hands on the table and looked at her. She stared back vacantly. "Your mother and I are getting married. We're trying to leave in two weeks. Special weekend rate. Three days, two nights in Vegas. We wanted to have all this worked out before we left, within the family."

A garage door fell in my brain and squashed a sleeping cat. I blinked my eyes.

"You what?"

"You heard me."

"No way."

A searing hurt ripped through me. My breathing shortened. A taste of panic rose in my mouth. Nancy sat in her vinyl chair like a yard ornament.

"I need a drink," she finally said.

Tears welled up in my eyes. I wiped them off with the cuff of my jacket.

"No way." I stared at her. "Marry this jerk?"

Lyle stiffened.

"The last thing you said about Lyle Cuff was that I should stay away from him. Now this." My voice rose as I spoke. And I suppose that I was beginning to sound hysterical, helpless like I was watching a dog die.

Nancy reached into the cabinet above the sink and collared a bottle. "I told you," she said, "to keep away from Lyle because he was drunk. I'd also made him mad."

"The asshole smacked you across the kitchen."

"That's enough." Lyle stood up and pointed that same stupid finger at my nose. "If you weren't my fiancée's boy, I'd have the Sheriff run you in. You're nothing but an ungrateful thief."

"She's not your fiancée, you asshole. She's my mother."

"Danny." She took a deep breath and faced us. It was like she was weighing something, maybe our relative atomic weight. "Danny, Lyle is right. He's trying to keep you out of trouble."

That's when I went blind. I jerked up the end of the table and shoved it into Lyle's pearl-buttoned western shirt. Lyle staggered backwards in his chair. The table blocked my way to him. I took a step towards Nancy. She winced like I was going to swing at her. That about killed me. The thought of hurting her hadn't crossed my mind, had never crossed my mind, not in my whole life. I just wanted the whiskey bottle. You know, some weapon to bash over Lyle Cuff's head.

As suddenly as it had begun, it stopped. I saw her scared and crying because of something I'd done, and I broke. Everything that meant survival just broke. The whiskey bottle was in my hand. I threw it against the wall over Lyle's head. I had no intention of hitting him. If I had, he'd have been cold cocked. He dove behind the table like a rat.

Nancy was sobbing, shaking. I pushed my way past her into the living room and climbed the stairs to my room.

I heard the door open, and Sheriff Douglas stomped back into the kitchen.

Lyle and the Sheriff talked, but I didn't want to hear their words. Didn't want to be a part of any of this anymore. I slammed my headphones over my ears and turned on the stereo. To this day, I have no idea what was playing. I waited for the Sheriff to come up the stairs and arrest me. I rolled up my sleeves so the cuffs would fit over my wrists.

There was more to this than a damn car.

From my window I watched the Sheriff leave the house, start his car. His headlights swerved out of the drive. A few minutes later, Lyle followed. Gravel spinning in a spray of bullets. Nancy was beside him in the passenger's seat. Elsie's Good Luck always had a booth for them. Coldest beer in town.

Only after they left did I go downstairs. For one thing to feed Merle, the second was to get a bottle of Valium out of the medicine cabinet. In the morning I needed to talk to Dale Reynolds about a car that had something illegal in the trunk. Just a hunch.

There's sometimes
a life within worlds
an onion of a world,
layer after layer
unfolding with tears.
Each night we
wash our hands.

26

Coach wrapped Angel's cast in foam rubber. He shifted him from starting quarterback to linebacker. The bum arm hung from his side like a club. The refs said he could play if he could handle the pain. Then they added, if the doctor says OK. Angel said yes on all counts. The doctor from the emergency room signed off. Well, he told Angel to avoid hard contact. Angel said sure. Then Coach Amber moved me to the other linebacker's slot. He suggested that I try not to get killed. I knew the position. Craig Morrison, the other starting linebacker, was sick with the flu. Lucky for me, I thought. Brian Murphy would step into the quarterback position. He did well there when we were winning by forty points. Amber was making do with what he had. November. End of the season. Wintry weather. Rain and mist and sleet in Kansas.

Lincoln High is out of Kansas City, a small school, a charter for inner city kids, smart as hell kids. But let me say that if anyone expected these guys to be a bunch of book worms and math geeks, forget it. They were tough. Hit hard. Coach said the game was all about smash-mouth football. Gator said that meant they were going to bring it to us with "physicality." That cracked me up. Five syllables. Physicality was the longest word I'd ever heard Gator use. Lincoln had two solid running backs, D1 prospects. One was a little wiry guy who ran like a track star. The other was a horse who loved to dive off tackle. It took two or three of us to bring him down. Their quarterback was only a sophomore, but he was solid. Their front line from tackle to tackle were Gator-sized. Solid, but not as mean and crazy.

So, what I'm saying is that our teams were evenly matched. As Coach predicted, it was a defensive struggle. Mostly on our side, because Murph was our quarterback. He lacked what Angel had . . . talent.

The first play from scrimmage. They sent their power running back, Number 35, right up the gut. The guard and center cut a hole through our front like a karate chop. Suddenly, he was two strides into a full out run and in my face. I dropped my shoulder and hit him in the stomach. Angel hit him at the same time from the right side. I was on my back about five yards down field with our entire backfield on top of me. I wobbled upright and Angel slapped me on the shoulder pads.

"Got'em, Danny," he said. Number 35 flipped the ball to the ref and bumped me as he jogged back to the huddle.

I lined up for the next play, still trying to quiet the bells in my head. Their quarterback took the ball from center and handed it off to Number 35 again. Our D-line crumbled. Same damn play. I lowered my shoulder, this time lowering my hit to his knees. Angel hit him from the right side again. I opened my eyes five yards downfield, still holding on to his ankles. Angel helped me up. "Got'em," he said.

"Got who?" I said through my facemask.

The next play, Coach signaled a linebacker blitz from the sidelines. The quarterback took the ball from center and faked a handoff to Number 35, who stood me up before I could wrap my arms. As I fell, once again five yards from the initial hit, I saw that their quarterback had pitched the ball around our weak side to Number 21. Good call. They'd suckèd us in. Number 21 took the pitch, turned up field along the sideline and ran alone into the end zone. Three plays.

Coach got in my face when I jogged off the field. "You got to get that guy, Prego. Number 35 is your man. Get that guy."

I thought I had.

"Each snap, son, you got to be on him. Each play. Where he goes, you go."

I nodded.

Angel was smoothing the tape back over his foam rubber.

"Chavez!" Coach yelled. "Same thing."

"It's going be a long night," I said to Angel after Coach had stormed off with his clipboard.

Angel grinned. "Eff him," he said. Coach Amber barked orders into Gator's helmet.

Eight long plays later. Dumb Murphy tossed a pass into the flat to Less Dumb Murphy, and we put our own six points on the board. Out of all the voices in the crowd, I could hear Mr. Murphy. "Way to go, boys!"

Mr. Murphy made me happy in a sad sort of way. He sat on the 50-yard line with a small group of other parents. Dale's dad. Gator's mom and dad. Gator's grandmother. Angel's father walked the sidelines with the chain gang. He ran the down's box.

My mother was at Elsie's. What the hell, I played football because I liked the game. I loved how the lights on a misty-ass night like tonight were self-contained, like a planet, like belonging, like time slowing down, like nothing else mattered.

Coach Amber's game plan became simple for me. My only assignment was to hit Number 35. The big kid had a name, Shock Edwards, just Shock to the announcer. Just 35 to me. Whenever he moved, I moved. Wherever he moved, I followed. By the second quarter he was all I could remember of the game. He ran the ball hard, but he'd begun to get fewer yards per carry. If he carried the ball, I stuck him as fast as I could. If he didn't run the ball, I still stuck him as hard as I could. My helmet began to learn the soft parts on his body: ribs, stomach, lower back, knees, shins. If I couldn't get to him, Angel or Gator did. I had one goal and that was to leave a bruise, no matter how large. Just before half-time, I speared him in the ribs after the whistle blew the play dead. Not intentionally. It was a matter of momentum and inertia. Shock yelled in pain, grabbed me by the helmet, and swung me ten yards across the far hashmarks. The ref threw his yellow flag. Unsportsman-like contact. Lincoln. 35 went crazy. I jogged back across the scrimmage line with a smirk on my face.

Gator gave me a high five. Not that it was a key play, just defense getting in 35's head. When the half ended, the score was 12-6, Lincoln. The coaches kept both teams under their goal posts during half-time. A small school thing. The locker rooms were across a cow pasture, through the parking lot, and across the gym floor. That meant taking off our cleats. Instead, we sat in a circle under the lights and tried to ignore the band as it crisscrossed the field. They played "Twist and Shout" for the pom-pom squad. Amber snapped at us and said to keep our heads in the game, not in watching the pussy. Frankly, my neck hurt too bad to turn it. All I could do was keep my eyes straight ahead on Dale Reynold's sweaty ass crack. Even in the November chill he was sweating like a dog. Only dogs don't sweat. They pant. Well, Dale was panting, too.

The second half began as a repeat of the first. We had the ball first and Dumb Murph threw a pass to Less Dumb Murph who was back behind the line of scrimmage. Less Dumb Murph floated one to his brother who'd darted downfield. He caught it on the 10-yard line and scrambled across the goal line with two Lincoln defenders on his back. The next series— Number 35 led off tackle as a blocking back for Number 21, Jamie Mears. 35 lowered his helmet into my helmet and my lights flickered. He went down hard. I went down harder. Gator, double-teamed, rolled up like a tarp. Angel followed Mears down the field, but it was simply a gesture of pride. No one could catch 21 once he headed south. Lincoln 18, Cliggett City 12. Points after were an issue. Neither team had a place kicker. Gator stuffed Lincoln's two point conversions. They stopped ours with a stacked line. Neither team had a placekicker who could kick on a wet field. The small school game plan was to run. And if that failed, run again the next time. It was simple. Simple as losing.

27

In the final minutes of the fourth quarter, Lincoln brought the ball down into our red zone. The clock drained away into the night. During the last sequence of downs, Gator had been double teamed at nose. His lungs heaved like a bellows. The last few carries had all been to their big man, Number 35. He'd slammed us for three-, four-, and five-yard gains. Alternating off left tackle, then right tackle, then left tackle again. Gator wasn't even getting to his feet. He crawled on his hands and knees from left side to right side and back again. Angel and I were filling the gaps. Hitting as hard as we could. Not only was the foam rubber on Angel's cast frayed, but the cast itself had begun to disintegrate where it crossed his hand above the wrist. His forearm shivers had stood blockers upright, but they were taking their toll on the plaster, not to mention his arm.

On fourth down, we called our final timeout. We took a knee in the icy mud between the hashmarks. Only Angel stood, hands on his hips.

"This is the game," he said. "Stop 'em here. We get the ball."

"Stop 'em," Gator yelled.

Angel looked over at me. "They're coming for you, Danny. Three yards is all they need."

I nodded. Spit through my facemask.

"Fake to 35?" I asked.

Angel looked toward the opposing huddle. "Good guess. Fake to the big guy, let Mears follow him in."

"Same as before," I said.

"Same as before," Angel said, turning to look at the clock.

And it was the clock I watched. When Lincoln lined up at scrimmage, 35 didn't take his eyes off me. No deception. I knew. So did Angel. Center hiked the ball to the quarterback. The quarterback swiveled at the hips, played a good fake. 35 doubled over as if to protect the ball.

Angel and I jumped early. We knew the cadence. No secrets. I hit 35 at the scrimmage line with every ounce of my 140 pounds. My helmet, aimed for his crotch, found its mark. Big boy hmphed and crumbled on top of me. Angel was a half-step behind me. He clothes-lined 21, swinging what was left of his cast like a battle axe. He caught Mears in the chest, wrapped up, and flung him back behind the line of scrimmage. On his hands and knees still, Gator buried him in a sweaty bear hug. The ref's whistle blew the play dead, I lay on my back with my arms around 35's thighs.

Already our offense was running onto the field to take possession. As I untangled myself from the big running back, Shock started laughing. Then I heard Angel laugh. The three of us slipped trying to stand and were instantly back on our knees. 35 said, "I feel like I'm a hundred years old."

"You're one ass-kicking grandpa," I said.

He rapped me on the helmet with his knuckles and we stood up. All except for Gator who was picking mud and grass out of his teeth. Angel and I stood over him. "I got smash mouthed," he said.

With less than a minute remaining, Dale and the Murphy brothers squeezed in three plays and a long Hail Mary. But that's where it ended, a last-ditch pass, batted to the ground by a Lincoln defender. The ball bounced alone into the endzone. Lincoln danced under the lights.

BINGO JESUS

28

ootball was finished. According to Angel, I'd played enough to earn my letter. One day I'd find a way to buy a jacket, deep blue with white trim. Nancy said on Sunday that she and Lyle were flying to Vegas sooner than she thought. Then she left in the car for Lyle's. I retreated to my room and listened to the sleet peck the window. Merle sat on the sill licking his front paw. I scratched his neck and he arched his back. I needed to talk to my dad. Even if he was dead, standing by his grave in his old boots in his old field jacket felt right, necessary. Screw school. Lyle. Nancy. I'd leave tomorrow.

Nancy didn't come home until Monday evening. I took her keys. The Gremlin had less than a half tank of gas. I didn't know if that was enough. Most of my travel experience was with the football team. Once I drove out of the range of league schools, I knew nothing. Knowing nothing was not new to me. I could know nothing with the best of them. I drove without a roadmap, threading my way through small towns, spotted along the highway with nothing more to mark them than a grain silo.

The National Cemetery was in Ft. Scott. Not a long drive, but I was penniless. Driving towards the state line, I felt better. I kept my eyes on the road, knowing that at the end of this long stretch was my dad. Cliggett City fell into a haze. You could say that there was just too much there for me to think about, so I sort of just gave it up. And as I drove, I didn't think, and I didn't feel, and not feeling was OK. Like becoming all gray inside. Better yet, blank like a TV set when you pull the plug.

The Gremlin sputtered down the highway, the only radio station for miles blaring hog futures through a single speaker. The fuel gauge bounced on empty. A road marker said *Arcadia ten miles*. And I had to laugh out loud. I'd never been to Arcadia, but I'd heard of it, and the way it was a Greek heaven on earth. We'd just studied the Greeks in mythology. Arcadia, a footnote.

No space between the E and the needle when I coasted in sight of Greek paradise. It rose out of this little hill between two horizon lines. Nothing special. A grove of trees with a few rooftops sticking out from them. A church without a steeple. And, of course, a grain elevator. The highway creased the edge of town, the railroad following alongside. Next to the highway was a gas station and quick stop grocery like the Easy Shop. The business district was to the north. I could tell that because of a sign that said *Bingo Bingo Bingo* and an arrow that had once pointed towards the center of town was now broken off and pointing up towards the North Star.

> *I almost wrenched my neck looking up.*
> *Like maybe Zeus was staring down at me*
> *with a you-finally-made-it-grin.*
> *The engine sputtered and died*
> *as the Gremlin coasted into Kansas*
> *heaven.*

Gravel crunched under the tires as I rolled to a stop at an old drive-in diner. The windows were boarded up. The door padlocked. I braked the Gremlin and got out, making sure to lock the doors. I had all my possessions in that car, crammed in a duffel bag. I pocketed the key and headed north at the intersection. I had driven into evening. The sky drained to darkness. I wasn't surprised that I'd run out of gas. Hindsight said I should have found money in Cliggett City. Begged. Stolen. Sold Merle.

The idea of taking the TV or my stereo and pawning it didn't cross my mind until I was well on the way east. There were boxes of Lyle's crap stuffed under the stairs. The stash was growing. CB radios was the newest thing. That and KitchenAid mixers. However, there weren't any pawn shops in Cliggett City anyway. I would have had to have driven over to some bar like Elsie's Good Luck and hit up the drunks, and now that Lyle was on the way to becoming my stepfather and co-owner of everything in our house, I doubted that he'd want to buy his own stolen mixer.

I found myself farther, further
than I'd ever been from home,
not just lonely, homeless lonely.
Too real the thought of nightfall
with nowhere to sleep.

29

There was still twilight to see by, but the incandescence from the houses was brighter, warmer looking even. Back in Cliggett City, I could walk Tomato Road on Saturday night and pretty much know everybody on either side of the street. I don't mean know them like a friend, but how you might know somebody in a newspaper.

In Arcadia, I was a ghost among shadows. I tightened the collar of my dad's field jacket around my neck, burrowed on to where a couple of streetlights had just flicked alive. If the Gremlin had gas, I would have turned around and driven as fast as I could back to Tomato Road and stuck my head under my blankets.

I took a deep breath and crossed the street towards a parking lot that also served as a basketball court. Some kid about my size was bouncing a basketball, shooting hook shots, missing even the backboard.

"Hey!" I yelled, waving my hand above my head like I was trying to flag down traffic.

The kid turned, and I could barely make out his face. He gave me a feeble wave, the way you do when you aren't sure if you should wave or not.

I stepped into the parking lot. It had also been painted like a tennis court. I didn't see any nets. "You live around here?" I asked.

He stared at me for a minute then dropped the ball and took off running around the corner of a laundry mat.

"Hey, wait a minute," I called after him. "I just wanted . . . "

I let my shoulder drop, not bothering to finish yelling into the wind. I crossed the parking lot and rounded the end of the coin-o-matic laundry, looking for some sign of the basketball kid. I ran into the Arcadia Women's Auxiliary.

A large woman with a pearl necklace and floral print dress met me in the middle of the sidewalk.

"You the fella scared Oscar?"

I couldn't tell if it was a statement or a question.

"Oscar?" I said.

"My grandson, Oscar. He was out here playing, said some man was following him."

"Oh, the kid shooting baskets. Yeah, I waved to him, but I wasn't following him. Just walking up from the highway."

"You're no grown man, either. You're just a youngster." She reached out a white gloved hand and turned my face into the light of the laundry sign. I pulled back.

"I'm in high school." The white gloves got me, just like this lady and her cronies were on their way to church. Not my usual crowd.

"You don't live around here, do you?" The lady was still peering at me like she was looking for dirt smudges on my face. At any minute I expected her to lick her thumb and give me a spit bath.

I cleared my throat. "No, ma'am. I'm from Cliggett City."

She looked at me down her nose. "I know Cliggett City. You alone or are your people with you?"

Two of the old women behind her began to whisper among themselves. I heard Cliggett City mentioned.

"I'm on my way to visit my dad."

"Where's he?"

I told her, thinking as I did that I wasn't exactly lying.

"I was driving my mom's car and it ran out of gas. I was looking for a gas station."

"Well, we got one, young man. But it's closed on Tuesday nights because of bingo. Double."

"Oh." I nodded my head like this made all the sense in the world. I didn't have a clue what she was talking about. It seemed that I was going to have to spend the night in the back seat of the Gremlin.

"Will they open early in the morning?"

"Six o'clock," said one of the ladies.

"Thanks." I turned, hoping to slip away from my interrogator.

"What's your name, young man?"

I probably should have lied, or made one up, but it's easier for me to lie to a cop than it is to lie to a plump aunt.

"Danny Prego," I said.

"Well, nice to meet you. I'm Martha Swenson and these ladies are Ray Ellen Jones and Sally Mock. Ray Ellen is the Grand Matron of the Arcadia Women's Auxiliary this year." They both squawked a chorus of hello and glad to meet you. Simultaneously. Martha Swenson smiled, her eyes twinkling like Seven-Up fizz.

"Glad to meet you."

"You've met Oscar." A sparrow peeked from behind the shoulder of the lady I guessed to be Sally Mock. She was the tallest.

Oscar waved.

I waved back.

"Oscar, why don't you take your friend Danny over to the bingo hall while we ladies have our palms read. Get him some of Bob Carl's chili. Nothing like chili, Danny, on a night like this."

Nothing like instant friendship.

When we came through the back door of the bingo hall, Bob Carl was hovering over this big steel pot, a cigarette dangling from his mouth. An old guy, an antique. He raised a spoon when Oscar introduced me, not taking his eye off the chili. The smell of garlic and onion filled the kitchen. My stomach gnawed itself from the inside out.

"Another stray."

I looked at him quizzically, not sure that it was me that he was referring to.

He must have read my confusion.

"I said, you're another stray." This time he took his cigarette out of his mouth so that I could hear him more clearly. "Martha and the girls are always herding in strays."

"I ran out of gas on the highway."

"That happens," Bob Carl said. "Got a name?"

I told him. He told me his. We shook hands over the chili pot.

"Out of gas, huh?"

"Yeah. I guess I was lucky, running out here in town. Gas gauge doesn't work well."

My mouth was salivating like a thunderstorm. I kept fighting back the drool from running out of the corners of my lips. It's not polite to slobber when you're getting acquainted, especially with old people.

Bob Carl removed a clean white bowl from a cabinet above the stove, ladled a huge spoonful of the chili into it.

"Well, one thing you can be sure of . . . " He thrust the bowl into my hands, the steam rising into my nostrils. "Long as you eat my chili, you're not going to run out of gas." He pushed a spoon into my hands. "Right, Oscar?"

Oscar grinned.

Bob Carl farted. "See what I mean?"

I laughed for the first time all day.

"Crackers are out on the tables. Get yourself a Coke out of the fridge."

Bob Carl's chili was nothing like I'd ever tasted before. When Nancy made chili, it was usually from a can with a little extra salt and pepper added. This stuff was in a football conference all its own. I was hungry enough to eat my boots if I'd had a little ketchup, so it didn't take much to curl my interest. Bob Carl cut up chunks of meat so that it looked like stew meat, only smaller. None of that hamburger stuff. He didn't use beans, just truckloads of spice. He called it Texas style.

I really didn't care what part of the country it was from. I just know it was deep red and fire hot. He said he added some extra zip to mine.

The bingo hall, as the old lady had called it, was also the place where you ate the chili. Made sense. I didn't have a clue about bingo, except for the kind we'd played in grade school. The room was about the size of an overgrown classroom. Maybe the size of the band room back in junior high. It was filled with rows of white topped folding tables and lined with those ugly metal chairs that every school in America owns. These had blue letters stenciled on the back that read *Ray Jones Mortuary*. They must have more need for bingo chairs than for funeral seats. I could get comfortable with that thought.

Oscar came in and sat beside me. He didn't eat but was sipping Dr. Pepper out of a can. He had this nasty habit of taking a drink and then licking the top of the can. I tried not to look, but I could tell right off that Oscar was the kind of kid you wanted to throw dirt clods at.

Martha Swenson returned from her palm reading session and told me that she'd given the matter of me some thought and she'd decided to do some checking. I must have frowned, because then she said she believed my story, but felt that it wasn't right for a boy my age to be traveling so far from home alone. In my head, I agreed. I mean if I had felt like I had much of a choice, or if I could turn the clock around, then I'd be back in Cliggett City eating a frozen pepperoni pizza and watching TV.

But like with Angel's broken arm and Saturday night's wild ride, once something's done, it's done, and there isn't any turning back. At least that's the way I saw it. When Martha Swenson said that she'd felt the need to check up on me, I had this sinking sensation that I'd been found out. Oh, I didn't let it show. I just nodded and said, "Yeah, that's OK." But it wasn't. She'd learned a lot from the palm reader. Bourbon on her breath. In her coffee.

Anyhow, I was developing a good poker face. That's what Lyle said one night to Nancy. Made sense to keep your feelings out of the picture. But what does a sixteen-year-old know? Martha Swenson sat down beside me at the bingo table and told me that she'd checked up on me by calling the Cliggett City police. Well, that meant Sheriff Douglas, because the Cliggett City police consisted of two cops who directed traffic after home football games. They only had one car. So, I knew she meant the Sheriff. I was done for.

She patted my arm. Her flabby triceps wagging in the bingo air like thick flags. "My boy was about your age when he took a notion to run away. This was years ago. Before times were dangerous like now. I was scared that something bad was going to happen to him. He didn't go far, just jumped a train and headed towards his grandmother's house. But Lord, I thought I was going to have a heart attack. I was so scared.

"You understand what I'm trying to tell you?" Martha patted my arm through my field jacket again.

"You think I'm running away?" I answered.

"A Sheriff Douglas reported you missing late this afternoon. He said you'd driven off in your mother's car and hadn't been seen or heard from for hours. You probably scared your mother and father to fits."

"My father's dead." I tried to sound as resentful as possible. I was angry with the old woman. She came across like a grandmother, or one of those aunts who sends you soap-on-a-rope every Christmas. But she was a snitch, a narc.

I balanced my spoon over my second bowl of Bob Carl's chili. "You tell the cops where I was?"

Martha sucked in some air like she was getting ready to bench press. "Yes, I did. If you and your mother have some differences then the best way to solve them is to talk, face to face." She took a sip of coffee she'd carried in a Styrofoam cup. She tipped the dregs into the trash and then called Oscar for a refill. Oscar licked the top of his can and disappeared into the kitchen.

"What kind of trouble are you in?"

I sat dumb. Not because I didn't want to talk, but just that I didn't have a guess as where to begin.

"Might help to get your problems off your chest."

Deep in my chest,
a willow branch
once twisted
behind barbed wire
sprung loose
and snapped into the air.

30

Yes, I did want to talk. I just didn't know how. Sounds stupid. But it's the truth, I didn't know how to talk about something that was buried deep. All the shit that had been piling up would take a backhoe to lift. Besides, I was pissed at this old fat busybody. What right did she have to check on me? Palm reader my ass. I sat for a few minutes and watched Oscar lick the top of his second Dr. Pepper can. I wondered if he ever cut his tongue on the tab.

Finally, I said, "I didn't exactly lie to you and your friends." I fumbled for the right words. "I really am going to see my dad, and I'm not running away. I'm on a road trip."

"Your dad? You said he's dead."

"That's right. He's dead and buried, and I've never been to visit his grave. Never. Not in my whole life. Things at home have been mixed up. Lyle's a jerk."

"Lyle . . . your stepfather?"

"Not yet."

Her head turned.

"Yeah. Stepfather, that's what he calls himself." I realized that she didn't have a clue who Lyle really was and that I wasn't giving a clear picture of what I'd been running from.

"Why the dislike?"

I couldn't believe she asked it that way. Not defending him, the way you might think one adult would do to protect another one. She was ready to believe me.

I told her. The whole story from Friday night. I even gave her the story about my dad and Vietnam. The whole thing. It was weird, but once I got started, I couldn't stop. We must have sat for some time because when I stopped, the bingo hall had filled. At some point Oscar brought Martha a fresh coffee and Bob Carl refilled my chili bowl.

Martha patted my hand and said that I should just hang around and we'd talk later. She also said if I wanted to walk out the back door and hitch a ride nobody would stop me. I smiled and gave her a big sure-enough with my white front teeth. Smiles keep old people relaxed.

I knew this one old lady back in Cliggett City who used to hire people for odd jobs on the basis that they were nice. If they could do the job only half-mattered. She seldom got suckered, but stuff like washing machines, lawn mowers, door latches were always falling apart. I guess that meant she'd rather hire a nice half-ass than a rude expert.

Martha threaded her way up to the little stage they had built next to the far wall and started to help Bob Carl pull bingo balls out of a spinning wire basket. There was standing room only. Oscar said that the bad weather was keeping everybody in. Meaning inside the bingo hall. He laughed.

Martha said to make myself at home, so I did. That meant picking up paper cups and finished bowls of chili. The Auxiliary kept dishing the red out and filling paper cups with coffee and Coca-Cola. Some were given special treatment from a silver flask.

My stomach was tanked to my uvula. I burped chili, enjoying the taste almost as much the second time as the first. I kept busy. There seemed to be no end to napkins and paper bowls. I stuffed them in plastic bags and then crammed the plastic bags in a big metal trash bin in back. Eventually, the lady I remembered as Ray Ellen Jones said they were running out of crackers. She sent me to her place to get more.

Her place was the funeral home. That's when I made the connection between the stenciled chairs and Ray Ellen. I stopped short and looked at her like I needed some more explanation. She clucked.

"That's right, young fellow. I'm the undertaker. Ray Jones Funeral Home."

I acted like it didn't matter one way or another. Crackers were crackers. But honestly, I'd never heard of a woman undertaker before.

Ray Ellen guessed that. She explained that her husband was Raymond Jones, and he was an undertaker too. They'd met at undertaker college or whatever. Her maiden name was Jones, the same. She said she liked the idea of not changing her last name after they were married. So she said yes when he asked.

Cool. But when I asked her if Mr. Jones would be home, she said that he was deceased. I said I was sorry (I was), but I couldn't help but wonder who'd embalmed him. You know, family discounts. She didn't elaborate.

The mortuary was only one block off Main. It was one of those ancient old Victorian homes that's too big for only two people, so it gets filled with dead ones, too. The back door was open. Didn't surprise me. I don't suppose many people, even hardened thieves, break into funeral homes. I slipped into the kitchen and under the cabinet by the sink was a big cardboard box of Stay Fresh crackers. I didn't get the pun until later. I shouldered the box and disappeared fast. I had this weird idea to peek into some of the front rooms, but they were dark. Darker than outside. I shivered.

Red lights whirled down by the highway where I'd left the dead Gremlin. I jogged down the road with the crackers under my arm like a football. My breath rose like a cloud.

31

The Gremlin was surrounded by highway patrol cars and a tow truck. Red lights reflected in the glass of the gas station and in the rain puddles that pocked the gravel lot. Like the Ginsburg poem. Ken Kesey. Hell's Angels. Surely, it wasn't so serious. Just an old Gremlin out of gas in Arcadia. I began to get the same creepy sensation that I'd felt in the funeral home. The cops were taking the car seriously, something criminal maybe. I swallowed, suspecting that in a few minutes they'd be looking for me as well.

My first thought was to slip out of town on the county road that intersected the highway. It disappeared into the darkness like a road to the moon, but the crackers banging against my ribs reminded me that Ray Ellen Jones had sent me on an errand. The errand turned me around. Not that I would really have walked off just like that with a case of Stay Fresh crackers. Plus, I didn't like the idea of being alone right then. The thought of all that nightfall pressing in on the lights of the town turned me back towards the warmth of the bingo hall. Sit in back and become invisible. Sink into the people the way the chili dipper sunk into the chili.

I had a lot of thinking to do. One thing was that tonight's bedroom was about to be towed down the highway. My duffle bag was still in the back seat. It wasn't late and I knew I had a whole lot of night ahead. Maybe I could hide behind the stack of bingo tables and wait till the lights went out. If I cut across the fields in the early morning, then got out onto the highway, I could hitch. I wanted to see my dad. One half of me wanted to make it to the cemetery, the other half was ready to give it up and ride home with the highway patrol. The ugly familiar is sometimes better than the haunting unknown. Damn, who's the palm reader now?

When I entered the back door of the bingo hall, Martha and Bob Carl were still calling out numbers; the Ladies Auxiliary clattered about the kitchen. I set the box of Stay Fresh on the stainless counter and slipped into a corner where I'd be out of the way. Ray Ellen was the only one who saw me, and she gave me a little wink. I'd barely calmed down when the front door opened, and two highway patrol officers walked in. Few did more than glance from their cards, except for Martha. She handed over the last bingo number to Bob Carl and made her way through the tables to where the cops were scanning the crowd. I slumped over a make-believe bingo card.

Martha greeted the officers like they were old friends. They shook hands, but I could tell she was wondering where I was because she kept rubbernecking the crowd. She led them to the kitchen. I skulked low in my seat when they passed, trying to look like the couple next to me, hunkered down, praying to the bingo god. When they passed, I stood up and walked to the front of the hall and out the front door.

The patrol officers still had their backs to me and were talking to Martha and Ray Ellen. They both saw me. Their eyes widened before the door shut.

32

Another patrol car was parked across the street. Two more officers sat inside with the dome light on. It looked like they were reading something on a clipboard. I must be some important criminal to attract two cars and four highway patrol officers. Or else it was a slow night in Kansas for criminal activity.

I snapped my jacket closed to my throat and walked where the shadows were deepest. I almost had it made when I scared a flock of pigeons that were roosting in the louvers of a lawyer's office. They flapped into the street, skimmed the top of the patrol car, and landed on the building on the opposite side of the street. The wing flutter caught the eye of one of the cops. He turned on his spotlight.

I broke into a sprint. An engine roared to life as I rounded the last building on Main. I ducked down one alley and then across a vacant lot, stumbling on a cardboard pizza box. I heard the patrol car's tires squeal behind me, gunning its four-barrel, stuck in a three-point turn in the alley, then it burst out between two buildings like a loose hunting dog. I leapt through a hedge and collapsed in the shadows, my chest heaving. The car slowed, flattening its spotlight on shrubs, fire hydrants, tool sheds.

I was back in the yard of the Ray Jones Funeral Home. I knew where there was an open door. *Déjà vu.*

I felt fortunate to make it into the back door, the way the spotlights were scanning the neighborhood like I'd escaped from prison. By the time I got in the door, even the neighbors were joining the cops.

Flashlight coins danced
on the clapboard siding.
Dogs barked. Cats meowed.
Birds fluttered up
from antique cedars
like bad dreams.

I squeezed in and hurried into a front room. I stood still until my breathing had calmed, my chest no longer heaving like a wounded animal. Waiting. One thing I knew was that I either had to turn myself in or get the hell out of Arcadia.

In the room to my left, I heard a clock ticking. Deep-throated like it had been ticking since the first clock, since Jesus was a little boy. It was both relaxing and eerie. I tried not to think about the eerie part. But the place gave me the creeps. I don't hang out with many dead people.

The back door opened.

Instinctively, I hurried low along the wall. Over in the far corner there was a red candle burning. The kind you see in churches and graveyards at night. Like a moth, I flitted over to it. I hadn't gone more than a couple of steps when I kicked a folding metal funeral home chair. It flipped against another one, and it against another. Like dominoes. It woke the de . . . Never mind, I won't say it.

33

A flashlight bobbed against the wall. I pressed my nose against the coffin drape.

A dead guy stared at the ceiling. Counted cracks in the plaster. Bald head shining in the red candle. Pink. Scrubbed.

"Look OK?" One of the cops asked.

There was a long pause; Ray Ellen was searching for something out of place. I knew the chairs had to be a mess.

"Must be your cat, Ray." This voice was Bob Carl's.

"I suppose . . ." Ray Ellen answered. "He must have crept in when we opened the door. That is unless Gaylord was up and around while we were gone."

The way everyone laughed I guessed that Gaylord was the bald dead guy in the coffin.

She flipped out the lights and Gaylord and I were left in the darkness. Up close the old guy smelled like chili powder and the biology lab at school, just before we dissected frogs.

I waited like a mole, quiet in my burrow behind the coffin skirt until the voices had vanished and the noises from the kitchen had died.

When I eased myself up, my left boot caught the fabric. As I turned, I stared nose to nose with Bob Carl.

"Boo," he said.

I collapsed back onto the floor.

Bob Carl laughed. He was doubled over and holding his sides like they were going to split.

"I came in to get you," he said. He laughed again.

"Very funny," I said.

"Be careful, kid. You keep this up and you're going to kill me."

I shook my head.

He took my elbow and guided me out of Gaylord's final bedroom and into the kitchen. I blinked at the brightness of the lights, and involuntarily stepped back into the sitting room.

"They're gone, boy."

I hesitated.

"Ray Ellen sent them down the road towards the highway. The highway patrol thinks you're hiding by the city park."

"Why'd she tell them that?"

"Well, the Ladies Auxiliary want us to get a running start."

"A what?"

"You want to see your daddy's grave, don't you?"

I nodded.

"Well, you got a chance, if you go with me, now."

"You'll take me?"

"My place is a bit down the road in Pittsburg. I'll drive you to Ft. Scott in the morning. Far as I know, you've done nothing wrong. Ask me, I say you just needed a ride."

I wasn't sure what to say. I couldn't see any reason why anyone would want to help me. Especially an old guy that I didn't know.

"You got to agree to one thing though."

I waited.

"When you get done paying your respects, you let me take you back to Cliggett City. They towed your car anyway. Turn yourself in and get this mess you're in cleared up. Go to school, play football, chase girls. Don't run around two counties with the state police force on your tail."

I stared at the linoleum.

"You agree. We go to visit your daddy's grave, then it's back home."

34

I fell asleep that night in Bob Carl's back bedroom feeling clean like I'd made a stay-fresh start.

Proud of myself,
the best-looking kid
at the orphanage

When morning came, Bob Carl had to wake me up. He had coffee in a big thermos and egg sandwiches on toast wrapped in wax paper. He'd put them in a black lunch box, the kind old men carry to work, and we ate them in the car as we drove out of town. The sun was just starting to turn the horizon pink, curved like an umbrella.

Bob Carl made a mean egg sandwich. The toast was covered with butter and the egg was seasoned heavily with pepper. In fact, it tasted like it had been fried in bacon grease, only I didn't get any bacon. Bob Carl ate it before I woke up. But he wrapped the sandwiches and brought them along for me.

When I bit into the toast, a spurt of yellow egg yolk burst onto the wax paper and ran down into my lap. I didn't notice it until it had dripped onto my jeans. Bob Carl tossed me an old red rag he kept under the seat of his car. One of those that mechanics use, a good napkin, even if it did smell like oil.

35

We drove into the cemetery at Ft. Scott about the time I'd have been catching the school bus back home. Row upon row of tombstones, small flat slabs curving the hill, stretching to the tree line. Quiet hung in the air. The main office wasn't open, so we sat in the parking lot under the bare limbs of a tree. We waited in the early gray, like for a dentist's office to open. I hadn't been nervous until Bob Carl drove into the parking lot and shut down the motor on the Oldsmobile.

One of them. My father's.

Bob Carl had a lot to say while driving, but once we stopped it was like he ran out of conversation. It was awkward. Finally, I asked him the question that had been bugging me all night.

"Why? Why help me?"

Bob sat at the steering wheel. He stroked the whiskers that were sprouting from his chin. Sparrows leapt from the office sign to the door. For a minute, I thought he didn't hear me.

"What would you do if you was me?" he asked. "Would you do things differently? You see some kid down on his luck. You ought to help. But you figure it's none of your business what the kid does. Then again, you know you could do a little. Maybe make a difference. So, what do you do?"

I tucked my chin down into my jacket collar. Remembered Franky.

"I try," I said.

Bob Carl nodded. "You try. You think one little push might be all this guy needs. You give him a meal. A ride. An ear."

"What if it doesn't do any good? What if this guy had stolen all your money or your car or your chili recipe?"

Bob cackled like a rooster. "Chili recipe, my ass. There ain't no recipe, except what's in my head. Hell, boy, you'd have to steal my brain. Better to make a mistake in someone's favor than against them. Trust, till you find out you can't. It's in the Bible."

It wasn't.

"Do Mrs. Swenson and Mrs. Jones feel the same as you?"

"Martha felt obligated to take you back home. She doesn't see that the quickest way home means a trip to Ft. Scott first." He chuckled. "Ray Ellen. This was her idea."

Finally, a copper-colored Mercury parked in the *Reserved for Office* parking space. A lady about Bob Carl's age got out. She gave our car a once over and unlocked the office.

"Bet that's our girl," Bob Carl said. "Nice legs for an old goat."

"Our girl" gave us a polite hello, then ignored us for the next five minutes while she put on a pot of coffee and swept out the floor onto the little back porch. She reached into a cupboard and shook a sack of cat food into a small bowl by the door. The water bowl looked empty, but she nudged it with her toe and water slopped on the floor.

I examined the graves. Shot with a surveyor's transit. It took my breath away to see them framed through the backdoor, to know that each one belonged to someone who had died. Somewhere was one with my dad's name on it. I felt part of something bigger than myself. My eyes clouded with water. I feared that a tear was going to leak out of the corner of my eye, so I turned around and stared at a plaque on the wall.

"Now, can I help you?"

I stared at the plaque.

"Danny?" Bob Carl's voice broke into my daydream.

"Yes," I whirled and found the two of them staring at me. "You can help me. I'm looking for my father's grave." I tried to sound mature, like I asked important questions like this all the time, but my voice broke and squeaked an octave higher than I wanted.

"Have you visited us before?" The lady smiled and tugged on her gray suit jacket.

I thought that was a dumb question. If I'd visited the cemetery before then I'd know where my dad's grave was. Wouldn't I? It was also the question that I had hoped to avoid. How bad is it when a dead guy's kid doesn't visit his grave? I felt about two inches tall.

I smiled and gritted my teeth. "No. This is my first visit."

The lady smiled.

"What's your father's name?"

"Prego. Anthony Merle Prego." I spelled it for her.

"I'll look him up in the register."

a book of names,
dead
to the sun, printed
in a permanent phone book.

I wished for flowers, a flag
to put on a grave.
Even the small flag
kids wave on the Fourth of July

36

I hadn't thought about flowers or flags at all. I was unprepared. The lady whisked through pages of names, a city of them. It dawned on me that I didn't know what I was going to do when I stood in front of my dad's cross. What are you supposed to do? I'd feel dumb saying a prayer out loud. Something more was called for. Maybe I'd just tell Bob Carl that I wanted to be alone and stand there by myself. I mean it was my father. We deserved some privacy after all these years. I hoped Bob Carl wouldn't be offended.

"What year was your father interred?"

"Pardon me?"

"Buried," Bob Carl answered. "When was your dad buried?"

I didn't understand graveyard talk very well. Yet, I knew that answer as well as my first name. "December 7, 1968." The words stumbled out. Nancy told me that much for a family tree I had to do back in grade school.

The lady turned to another book and began to shuffle through more pages.

"You want me to wait out in the car?" Bob Carl asked.

"No. I may need to remember directions. This is a big place." I was impressed by Bob Carl's politeness.

"Sure is," Bob Carl agreed as he gazed out the window.

"Young man," the lady said. "We don't have an Anthony Merle Prego listed with us. We don't have any entrees with the name of Prego."

"What do you mean?"

"I've looked the register over, cross referenced the date. There is no Prego in the National Cemetery."

I spelled his name for her again. "Corporal. United States Marine Corps. He was killed in Vietnam by friendly fire in December of 1968. He was buried here in the National Cemetery. My mother came to the funeral."

"Young man, you were just a little boy in 1968. You really think you could remember that clearly? You may have been mistaken about the location. There are other cemeteries in town, other National Cemeteries in the state."

"No. I'm sure it's this one. Nancy described the white crosses. The honor guard folded a flag and then a bugle blew *Taps*. She told me about it. I was sick or something when he was buried so she left me with the neighbors for a couple of days. Nancy said . . ." I turned and faced the window, not finishing what I was going to say. The tombstones, shields, were a blur. A ringing in my ears. I stared into the gray mist. White crosses. "She said white crosses."

"Danny, could it be that he was listed under another name. I'm Bob, but my birth certificate has me listed as Robert." He had a hold of my arm.

"Italian names were often changed when immigrants came through Ellis Island." She paused. "You like to use the phone? Maybe you could call someone who would know."

"She said white crosses."

"You can call collect." The lady inched the phone closer to the edge of the desk.

"Danny. Those aren't crosses," Bob Carl said.

I pushed open the door and rushed into the gray morning. A clip of sun in the east burned through another lie.

37

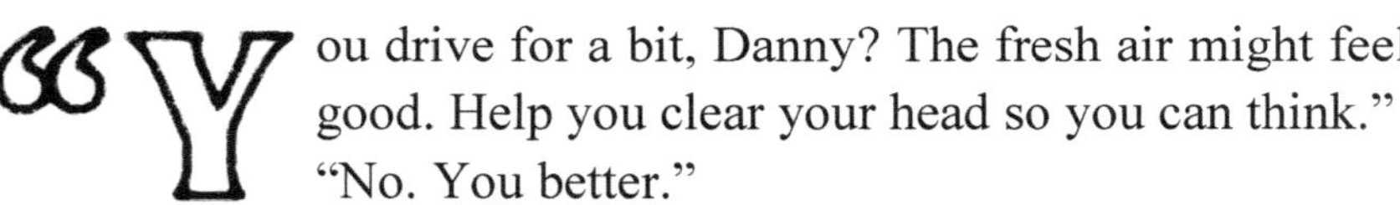

ou drive for a bit, Danny? The fresh air might feel good. Help you clear your head so you can think."

"No. You better."

Only minutes ago, I was alive with pride over my father the war hero, and now I was being told that he wasn't buried where Nancy said. Twelve years is a long time to be misled. Lied to.

"Let's go," I said.

I tried to remember my last conversation about dad's burial. Nancy said how special it was to see his white cross among all those other white crosses. And the honor guard. And the flag. But there were no white crosses. No honor guard. No flag. Tombstones. Like the Ten Commandment tablets.

The sun retreated. Mist turned to rain. I could feel cold spray on my face and hear it splatter my dad's field jacket. In the reflection of the car window, I saw my tangled hair. The jacket pulled to my chin to keep out the cold. I'd never noticed it before, but above the pocket was a dark strip where a patch had been removed. A couple of green threads were still tangled in the fabric.

"Don't these coats usually have names on them?" I asked Bob Carl.

128

He thumped the dark, empty spot above the pocket with his knuckle. "Yeah, right there."

Bob Carl's Oldsmobile droned down the highway. I was quiet as a knob on the door. There was nothing to say. I apologized to Bob Carl for all the trouble I'd caused him. He shrugged me off. We'd driven maybe halfway back to Arcadia when I said it again. Said I was sorry for the mess, the drive, the money spent on gas. Again, he waved me off like he didn't want to hear any apologies. He leaned across the seat and whispered out of the corner of his mouth that families were seldom simple. That's all he said.

I heard him.

Another major screwup involving my family. My dead father couldn't even get killed and buried right.

Maybe Dad was killed by the real enemy. Maybe he was buried in Cliggett City and Nancy was just too drunk to remember. Maybe the mistake was my fault. Maybe I was such a bad kid that Nancy had begun drinking and dad ran off to get killed rather than face me. And this was the bomb. I could have screwed the family up. Franky could do better than me.

I closed my eyes and pressed my head against the window. Sleep wasn't fair to Bob Carl. He was as tired as I was. I should have stayed where I belonged. I rocked, quietly, the highway thumping below the tires. I prayed to God that he'd open a hole in the earth, and I'd drop in it. Open the car door. Fall out on the highway. I took some satisfaction in imagining myself flopping across the pavement like a doll. I eased my hand to the door handle, the cool metal in my palm like a gun. It comforted me, the thought, opening the door, dropping. Bombs away.

But I didn't. Falling out of a car door at sixty miles per hour wasn't a sure thing. I probably would have just bounced along for a while and then rolled to a stop, paralyzed like a vegetable, a potato. Where would I be then? Certainly worse off. Bob Carl knew I was feeling terrible. About thirty miles down the road he asked if I wanted a chocolate shake. We were passing through

Pittsburg. Miles from Cliggett City with a kid who was thinking about offing himself.

How crappy would he feel if the kid he was trying to help suddenly threw open the car door and cracked his head open on the no passing line. Mashed potato in the middle of the road. He'd have this terrible mess on his hands, roadkill to explain, then he'd have to live with this dead teenager in his head for the rest of his life.

I didn't want a chocolate shake, but he bought me one anyway at the Pittsburg Ice Cream Company, a small white building off Broadway. "Good stuff," he said. "I found this place in college."

The waitress, as pretty as Beth, counted back Bob Carl's change. She wiped the counter. Bob Carl handed me the extra penny.

"Put it in the gumball machine. If you get a spotted ball, you win a quarter."

I dropped the penny in the slot. Cranked the handle. The gumball clanked down the chute. It was blue.

"Next time," Bob Carl said.

Tears came to my eyes.

"Here, take this." Bob Carl handed me a long plastic spoon. "Too thick to drink through a straw."

> *the more I spooned*
> *the chocolate shake, the more*
> *the beanfields began*
> *to color around the edges*

MERLE JOINS THE FBI

38

Merle the Cat jumped out of the dirty clothes hamper and crawled up in my lap. I rubbed the scruff of his neck. He dug his nails into my thigh. "Ow, you shit," I said, tossing him onto the punched pillow. He curled into a ball and licked his paw.

I took a deep breath and looked at the clock. It was only a little after six. That meant that I had the whole night ahead of me to put my life back in order. I'd had the same clothes on for the past two days, so I took a shower, washing my hair twice, letting the hot water smooth out the knots in my neck. The clothes I put on were clothes that I'd stuffed in my duffel bag, ones that had been carried off in the Gremlin when it was towed back to Cliggett City. It took a while to find the least wrinkled shirt, but I finally found a maroon flannel and a second pair of jeans. Socks weren't so easy, but I dug a pair from under my bed. Underwear was a lost cause, so I just wore an old pair of gym shorts. Sometimes I don't wear underwear. Commando. It's not like anybody's going to notice. With my luck I'll probably fall in love with some beautiful waitress, and then right in the middle of a date, my pants will rip . . . faded red gym shorts.

I left the house, walking the hedgerow to intersect County Road. That was the shortest way to Elsie's Good Luck. I wanted to face Nancy. Bob Carl had dropped me off two hours ago. The house empty. The floor furnace cold. I had his phone number. Promised to call.

I wanted to face her before she got drunk. Bob Carl agreed.

I was too late. When I spread the barbed wire, my jacket dripping with November mist, I could see Lyle's El Camino parked in front. It was the closest car to the front door. I expected to see a little sign on the parking place that read *Nancy Prego, Danny's mother. Most Loyal Patron.* But it was just a parking space, and when the car was gone, there was only darkness until another car filled the space. No honors for drunks, not even for mother-drunks.

The dome light was on in the El Camino. Someone had parked in a hurry, eager to get at it. Nancy was careful about dome lights. In the daylight Elsie's is a dump, just a squat little brown building with a flagstone veneer by the front door. It had two long windows in front, windows heavy with neon beer signs. No windows on the sides. An air conditioner leaned out of one wall. A maze of beer boxes, trash cans, and a bent metal shed lined the back wall. An over-sized couch had been dumped in the trees. Outdoor seating.

Jacket collar against my neck, I walked across the highway, boot heels on the blacktop. When I got to the El Camino, I bumped the driver's door with my hip. It shut, snuffing out the dome light. Even if it was Lyle's car, there was no sense in killing an innocent battery.

One of the cars in the parking lot was a GTO. Gator. I hesitated at the door. The thought of saying something emotional to Nancy in front of friends is Valentine sweet, but this wasn't about sweet. More like Groundhog truth. The future.

Elsie's is always dark. Too dark. Even in mid-afternoon, the only lights are the beer signs that line the walls. Sometimes the pool table glows with the Falstaff sign above it. That helps. The place was more crowded than it looked from the road. I stood by the door trying to recognize faces through the cigarette smoke. When you're underaged, you don't want to come bouncing into a bar like you just got off a school bus.

In my case, the owners knew me well. I'd been in attendance since elementary school. I used to do my homework at the table that was the most lit up by the video games. Still, I kept myself low-key, invisible.

Gator played pool with Nancy. She tossed her hair like a schoolgirl as she chalked the cue, speaking more with her eyes than with her mouth. He pretended to be more interested in the stripes than in her. I had to admit that in the bar room light she was in her element, free-spirited, momentarily transported. Gator would have crapped if he'd known she was old enough to be his mother, too. On second thought, Gator wouldn't have cared.

I stood there for a minute with my hands in my pockets, the water from my jacket dripping onto the floor. Nancy balanced a cigarette on the rail, laughing about her near scratch. She put her hand on Gator's arm like they were old friends. Took a puff of her cigarette and blew a long slow stream of smoke into the pool table light. That's when she noticed me standing by the *Coldest Beer in Town* sign. She stopped in the middle of a shot and stared at me. Gator grinned through the beer.

"Danny," she said. "What are you doing here?" She picked a piece of tobacco off her tongue and flicked it into the darkness.

I cleared my throat. "I came down to talk to my mother." I put a little emphasis on the *mother*.

Gator heard, but it took a few seconds for it to sink in. Blank, like a parking meter that had just run out of time. It clicked. "Your mother?" he said.

"Hey, Gator," I said. "Yeah. Nancy, this is my friend from school, Gator. And Gator, this is my mom from birth. Nancy, Gator. Gator, Nancy."

Gator tried to act like this was the most normal introduction in the world. Shooting pool and flirting with a teammate's mother was just as normal as a laundromat. But I could see his eyes—he'd been caught where he shouldn't be. I was embarrassed for him, pissed as well. How many of my friends had mothers who acted like pick-ups in rundown bars? I knew of only one.

"You want to shoot my turn?" Gator asked, leaning the cue towards me.

"No thanks," I said.

Gator leaned his pool cue against the table. "You guys talk." Then he headed towards a booth in the back. The one that was darkest where Elsie couldn't see how young the drinkers were. "You come on over and sit down with us if you want." Gator added before he plopped down in the booth. It looked like he was sitting with Dale and the Murphy brothers. They hadn't looked up until Gator scooted them over. Somebody waved a pale hand in the Coors sign. I nodded.

She turned her back on me and walked over to the bar to get her beer. I followed.

"Where's Lyle?"

She shrugged, still not turning around to face me. "Don't know. Don't care."

"A change?" I asked, hoping he'd fallen in front of a chicken truck.

"One of his moods." She squashed her cigarette in the ashtray. "When he's like that, I don't care if I ever see him."

"You leaving him?" I knew I'd spoken too quickly.

"Mind your own business." She turned and looked at me. "You shouldn't have run off."

"Yeah." I said. "You shouldn't have done a lot of things, too. My father was one. Want me to go on?"

She glared at me for a second and then reached into her purse.

"What do you need, Danny?"

I didn't like the way the conversation was going. I could tell that this was not a good night to talk. But then, when was it ever?

"I walked over here, not to argue or bitch about your life. I just wanted to tell you that I think I can understand why you made up the story about my father."

She stiffened her back like a cat. "There's no way you could know."

I didn't flinch. Knowing this wouldn't be easy from the start. I looked her straight on.

"You were a kid."

"Seventeen."

A tear? I couldn't tell. She turned and brushed something back with her hand. The one that held the beer bottle by the neck. It was like she was listening to the jukebox.

"Why, Nancy?"

There, I'd said it, straight out without any qualifiers or hidden messages. Just a plain ass question. My voice arched across the empty barroom air like smoke.

She lowered her head and then lit her cigarette with her Bic. She took a hit and shook the hair out of her eyes.

"Dan . . ." she started to say, when her eyes narrowed at the doorway behind me. "Shit. The asshole's back."

Lyle was leaning to the south. He staggered. I'd seen his drunk walk a lot of times. He rolled across the floor like he was on the deck of a pirate ship, a character in *Treasure Island*. But with Lyle, it wasn't the walk that identified his moods, it was the tilt of his head, the switchblade eyes. That was obvious as soon as he stepped into the light of the revolving beer sign. The one that showed this running river one moment and then a quiet lake the next. There was only a hole where the name of the beer used to be. A recent addition.

Lyle glared at Nancy. He removed the beer from her hand and took a swallow. He swished the amber around the bottom of the bottle.

"Saved me the backwash, huh?"

She rolled her eyes. "Didn't know you were coming."

Lyle held the empty up into the light so that Elsie could see that he wanted another.

"Guess I take care of everything."

"Guess so," Nancy said flatly. She motioned with her eyes for me to move out of the way. But I was too slow.

Lyle finished off her beer and turned to face me. There was hatred in his eyes. The kind of hatred a man saves for special moments in his life. But his voice came out syrupy.

"You're back. Danny Boy's back from the big world." He put his arm around my neck, and let it hang like a noose. He pulled me towards his face.

"You OK, son?" He emphasized son.

I winced and tried to back off a step. Lyle tightened his grip.

"What's the matter? Living with your mother and me not good enough. You steal our car. Go running off to . . . where did you say that he run off to?"

"Leave the boy alone, Lyle. He's done nothing to hurt you. What's happened is between him and me."

"Between him and me." Lyle smacked his lips, bringing his whiskered face down only inches from my nose. His breath reeked with alcohol. "His daddy. That's what you said, Nancy. He went off to find his dead daddy's grave. That right, son? How'd that go for you?"

Lyle was resting most of his weight on my shoulder and it was getting hard to keep my balance. His breath turned my stomach. I thought I was going to puke. If so, I could aim it down the front of his shirt. It would take all night to clean the chunks out of the grooves in his gold chain.

I shrugged out of his half nelson. He was off balance enough that he slipped and banged against the pool table. I danced out of the way and positioned myself by the juke, hands at my sides, arms bent at the elbows, knees bent like a linebacker. I could feel the rage of the past few days welling up inside. It felt good. Lyle, the focus for the past week, the past year. It was pure.

I motioned for him to come towards me. Kind of like you might wave a car onto a hydraulic lift. Lyle lifted himself up from the green felt. His eyes never leaving mine. The bar quieted and I heard Elsie say something like *damn damn damn.* Lyle stood himself upright, one hand on the pool table. He set his beer on the felt. It fell over. Beer pooled around the eight ball. He moved towards me, a trash truck in low.

Lyle pointed his finger the same way he did the night I aimed the BB gun at his nose. He wagged it like he was giving me some warning. "I'm gonna cream your ass," he said. "You've been needing what I'm going to give you for a long time."

"You're not going to touch him, Lyle." Nancy yanked Lyle's arm, swinging him slightly around to face her.

He shoved her into the bar.

I stepped to catch her.

Gator and the Murphy brothers pushed through the crowd. They squeezed around the pool table between us faster than Lyle could react.

"Get the hell out of my way, fat boy," Lyle yelled.

Gator didn't move. Neither did the brothers although they kept a step behind Gator. "You're drunk, Cuff," he said.

"Move your ass."

Gator held his own. I could see Lyle's eyes sizing up his chances of taking on all three. Possibly, he was drunk enough to try, but then his face relaxed. He threw up his hands.

"You stick up for your friend, don't you?"

Nobody answered.

Lyle took a deep breath, and then let it out slowly. "Man," he said, raising his head and staring at the ceiling like he was counting stains. "I sure do have a mean temper, don't I?" Then he lowered his gaze to meet Gator's. "I am glad you guys snapped me out of it." He held out his hand. "No hard feelings."

Something inside me wanted to scream, *watch out for a knife,* but Lyle's hand was empty. Gator took it.

The bar relaxed and everyone breathed.

"Damn you to hell, Lyle Cuff!" Elsie snapped from behind the bar. "You're going be the death of me."

"Sorry Elsie," Lyle apologized. Then he motioned for Gator and the brothers, "You guys come over here to the bar and I'll buy you a drink."

They looked at each other uncertainly. I started to say no, don't do it, but I didn't. They moved to the bar. Lyle saw me standing by myself by the door. "You too, son. Mostly you."

39

Nancy turned around and dug into her purse for another cigarette. She lit it and then tossed her hair back and fastened it with a rubber band. There was nothing but tension and worry in her face. Lyle's eyes still held their switch-blade gleam.

He bought two buckets of long neck Busch. That's a special Elsie runs where you get a bunch of cheap beer cheaper than if you bought them one by one. It commits you to drinking and saves elbowing to get back and forth through the crowd. After a few buckets, no one remembers who they were drinking with or which bucket to choose from. Nancy didn't join us. She sat at the bar talking with Elsie and one of the other female regulars. Gator and the Murphy brothers were laughing at Lyle's stupid jokes like they'd been friends for years. I hung on to one beer. I wanted to ask what had happened to Dale, but I had this feeling that he'd disappeared when Lyle came in. It had something to do with his *borrowing* a Chevy.

At nine-thirty, Lyle got up to go to the john. He'd kept his eyes on the clock like he was trying to figure out how to tell time. I was the only one who noticed that he stopped behind the bar and made a quick phone call on Elsie's private phone. I should have

141

known that meant something, but my head was starting to hurt. I let it slip.

Lyle rejoined us like nothing had happened, but I was suspicious. You don't hang around with snakes all your life and not get a feeling for when they're about to strike. Whenever Lyle smiled, I suspected trouble. Part of me said to grab my coat and get the hell out of Dodge. The other part of me said that if Lyle meant trouble for my friends, then it was my doing, and I should stick around. Responsibility, you know.

Lyle bought another bucket and thudded it on the table like an exclamation mark. Gator pulled two from the bucket for the Murphy brothers. They were wobbling in their seats. I wasn't sure how much they'd put away before I got there, obviously a few. Let's put it this way, they weren't in any position to tie their own shoes. They needed Velcro.

Lyle passed me a beer.

Gator slipped the end of the beer bottle into his mouth and popped it open with his front teeth. It was a talent of his, one I'd heard of, but never seen. The brothers cheered.

"Here, Chub, open mine too," Lyle said.

"The name's Gator."

"What's that?"

"I said the name's Gator, not Chub."

Lyle smiled. "Sure, sorry about that, buddy."

I knew he wasn't, but Gator seemed satisfied.

About this time, the door opened, and three cowboys stepped in. I'd seen a couple of them last summer at the chicken factory. A grin crept over Lyle's face.

"Hey, Chub, I'll tell you what," he spoke directly to Gator.

Even drunk, Gator looked at him with this surprised exasperation. He waited.

"Chub," Lyle continued, "how's about you and your friends step outside with me and my friends and we kick your asses across the parking lot? What do you think about that, fat boy?"

I cringed. Gator peeled his beer label. He turned the bottle in little circles on the wooden table. The Murphy brothers weren't responding very clearly. Brian was nodding to the music of Merle Haggard and Brad was watching Gator with slightly crossed eyes, chewing his bottom lip nervously.

"Sure," Gator said. "You and your friends meet us around back. If we're not there in five minutes, start without us."

Brad laughed nervously. You know, like he'd never heard it before, when it was one of the oldest jokes in history. The other brother broke into a grin as soon as it dawned on him that his brother thought something was funny.

Gator wasn't smiling. He didn't want any part of Lyle's friends.

"So, you're a funny boy," Lyle said, reaching across the table and poking Gator with his finger. Gator slapped his hand away like it were a gnat. Lyle stood up fast and grabbed Gator by the collar of his flannel shirt. I heard it rip.

"That's my shirt, you mother—" Gator said. In a second, he twisted Lyle's forearm down hard on to the table and Lyle came tumbling with it. Brad Murphy swung at Lyle's head and missed but knocked his Monroe cap into the face of the cowboy with the Carhartt jacket.

"Stop!" I swept the beer bucket off the table, bottles crashing across the floor, foaming in yellow swill.

Responsibility.

Gator leapt up. Even Lyle stopped. Eyes wide.

"Enough!" I said.

I brushed past Nancy and walked out the door. I was halfway across the parking lot when she caught up with me. "Your father left me." Her face contorted in pain. "He left with my best friend. Killed by friendly fire. I didn't lie. You happy?"

I wasn't.

She turned on her heel and walked back to Elsie's. She stopped before the door.

"He's in Nashville. Go find the asshole."

The door opened behind her. Gator and the brothers shuffled out into the parking lot. Brad held Brian up by his arm.

"You drive?" Gator said.

He tossed me his keys and I followed them to the car.

40

Dale Reynolds rolled a pencil-thin joint on Rita's spool coffee table. A candle, wedged in a wine bottle, burned in the center of the table. The curtains, drawn, glowed with a deep maroon light from the street. I joined Gator on the couch. Angel and Rita shared a frayed La-Z-Boy Recliner. Rita's cousin curled on the floor with her arms folded on Dale's lap. She smiled at me when I came in. I smiled back.

"Hey," I said.

"Hey," she said.

Dale lit the joint with an old Zippo. The flame turned the tip to a smoldering inferno. He held the smoke expertly and passed the joint to Gator.

"Where's the brothers?" Angel asked.

"Took them home." Gator exhaled. "Farm work tomorrow."

"Auction," I added. "They're going with their dad to a cattle sale."

I took a hit and passed the joint to Rita. She tossed back her hair and put the joint to her lips. A beautiful gesture. She passed it to Angel. A seed popped. Angel passed it to Candy on the floor.

The television on. The sound off.
Channel 4 News was at Willy's Truck Stop
out on Highway 7. The news girl
knotted her forehead as she talked.
She turned her body to show a semi
behind the gas pumps. Looked like
another hijacking. Gator nudged me,
stuck the joint under my nose.

"Can't you find cartoons or something?" he asked.

Angel shrugged. "I wanted to hear about Lincoln's game at State."

"Shit," Dale said. "The good guys lost."

Angel took the joint from Rita. "Rumors."

Gator rolled his head back. "35 was one hell of a back."

Candy dropped an ash into her lap. Brushed it to the floor.

"They kicked our asses," Dale said.

Nobody said anything for a few seconds.

"No," I said.

"No, what?" Dale said.

I took what was left of the joint between my fingers, pinning it with my fingernails. "Nobody kicked our asses."

Dale rubbed his temples. "Felt like it."

Angel leaned forward in the La-Z-Boy. "Danny's right. They beat us, but nobody kicked our asses. We could have played tonight with the right play, one more Hail Mary, a bootleg."

"True," Gator said. "They were happy, but the pain they felt. That's from us."

We liked that thought. Rita dumped the roach in the ashtray. "Beer anyone?"

We raised our hands.

She came back from the kitchen with a six-pack. The girl on the TV was interviewing some guy with a cowboy hat.

"Another hijacking. Just after dark," Rita said before squeezing in next to Angel again.

A tow truck sat off to the side of the screen, next to the Spicy Chicken Wings sign. A '57 Chevy hung from the hoist. "Hey, that's Lyle Cuff's '57," I said, looking closer. Everyone turned to look at the screen.

"Sure as hell is," Gator said. "I'd recognize that piece of shit anywhere."

"Well, at least the roof," Rita laughed.

"It'll never run again," Angel said.

I had to agree. Sunk in a creek doesn't help.

"Never supposed to work," Dale said.

We set down our beers and waited for him to explain. He sighed. "I didn't steal the car that night."

"What?" We said in unison.

Dale toyed with his beer bottle. "Lyle's my dad's friend. Business friend. Lyle brought the car over to the house with Sheriff Douglas. He said I could drive it to pick up a pizza at Casey's. My dad didn't want me to. But I did. I brought the pizza back and then Doyle Martin showed up with his tow truck."

"The one on TV?" Rita asked.

"Yeah. They unloaded a plastic bag from the back of the truck into the trunk of the '57. Then the phone rang inside, and they all went into the garage. When I drove by Martin's an hour later, the car was parked in back with the other junk." He paused and took a drink. "I still had the keys.

"They use the car to haul weed. Martin drives it around hooked up on the hoist just like any other tow job. If he's stopped, he has reasonable deniability. Something like that."

"Mexico?" Angel asked.

"I don't know," Dale said. "I just heard them talking."

"Your dad and Lyle?" I asked, floored by thought.

A pained expression crossed Dale's face. "I don't know. His lawyer. Maybe. I don't know."

"And so . . . you stole the drug car," Rita said.

"And so, I just took the car and drove off. I didn't know then what I know now."

"Jesus," Angel said.

"And you came by here?" Rita shook her head.

"Yeah. I knew you didn't have a ride. I thought we could drop the car off on the way to meet Gator."

"Christ, man!" Angel said. "You should have said something. A trunk-full of weed."

"Who leaves weed in the trunk of a piece of shit?"

Dale lowered his head and rested it on the top of his bottle. "I didn't know about the pot. Not then. But yeah, full of smoking dope."

"It was there for a drop off, a sale," Rita said. "It's smart."

"We almost got killed, asshole," Gator said.

"You think I don't know that." Dale raised his head. His face drawn, sad, a deflated football.

"Christ," Angel said.

Dale shrugged. "I know. I know. It was just too good, I thought."

"Good?" I asked.

"Yeah. I didn't think they'd get so pissy."

"Pissy!" I said. "You stole Lyle's pot."

"I didn't know until later. Overheard Lyle and Dad on the phone. Shit, Danny. I screwed up."

The room grew quiet. I could hear the termites in the walls planning their next meal. Dale looked at us all pitifully, his eyes like wet saucers. "I didn't start to figure it out until I got home that night. Sheriff Douglas was at the house. He and my dad were talking on the deck. Everything got blown out of proportion. They shouted. Douglas stormed off pissed."

"Douglas," I said. "Makes sense. He was with Lyle in Chicopee. He was with Lyle at my house Monday night."

"Smart," Rita said again.

I had to agree, but the damage was done. We sat around the table staring at our feet. Gator picked his teeth with his fingernail.

Finally, Angel moved Rita off his bum arm. "Tell you what, man."

Dale eyed him hopefully.

"Roll us another joint, and you're forgiven."

Gator clapped his hands. "Mercy of the court, baby."

Dale pinched the bridge of his nose. "Shit. This was all I had."

"Fix it," Gator said. "Go get some from Lyle."

My blood turned cold. I wanted no part of anything involving Lyle effing Cuff.

"Not a good idea," I said. "Not tonight."

"You drive." Gator dangled his keys from his middle finger.

41

Lyle owned acres off Highway 7. I'd never been there before, but Dale said his dad had driven him there to hunt doves. We drove two cars. Dale's 150 and Gator's. I drove the GTO. Gator said his head was still pounding, plus he insisted he was tripping on the smoking dope. I didn't argue. Rita snuggled with Angel in the backseat. They made out all the way out to the farm. Farm, my ass. Dale led in his truck with Candy up against him, glued together.

For me, I couldn't get Nancy out of my head. Standing outside Elsie's. Telling it straight. My dad, dead this morning. Now, alive in Nashville. I needed to talk to Bob Carl about this one. Maybe I had a bus ride in my future. Maybe this summer. I needed money. Should have stolen Lyle's pot. Driven to Chicopee. Sold it to the bowling league. The janitors who had to clean up chicken shit.

Dale drove the long way through the pits, the road winding the mined land like a snake. The pit water glittered under a dark sky. No moon, low clouds, still the spit of rain. Tree limbs hung over the road, bare, stretching down as if to touch the roof of the car. Gator had popped Credence into the player, leaned back and closed his eyes, nodding his head in time with the music. Through the rearview, Rita and Angel had slumped so far down in the seat that they'd vanished from sight. Not that I was spying. In front of me Dale swerved from one side of the dirt road to the next. Not fast like he was drunk, more like he was getting road head. Not that I was spying.

We crossed Highway 7 only a few miles north of the truck stop, then drove another section of dirt road. Finally, Dale slowed to a stop near a low water bridge. His door opened and he walked back toward us. As I expected, his shirt wasn't tucked in. Gator tapped me on the arm and grinned.

"You guys hang back at the railroad tracks. I'm going to drive in. Those guys don't like strangers showing up at all times of night." He leaned into my window.

"Don't you think Danny is a bit more than a stranger?" Angel said from the backseat.

Dale frowned, perplexed. "Sure," he said, "I just meant that . . ."

"It's good," I said. "I'll hang back."

Dale still grimaced, "I didn't mean he didn't know you," he said.

"No. Really, Dale. It's good. I mean it. Lyle hates my ass."

He scratched his head.

"Dude," Gator said. "Your pants are unzipped."

Dale jumped back and reached for his fly.

The GTO erupted in laughter.

"Pricks," Dale said.

We followed him to the railroad tracks, swinging off the road into a small cinder turn around.

Dale drove to the next drive, camouflaged by the hedgerow that ran next to the gravel shoulder. He braked and turned in.

"I want to see this asshole's farm," I said, surprising myself. I opened the door and walked the road in Dale's tracks. I was out before anyone could say a word. Behind me I could hear CCR on Gator's tape player, muffled, distant. "Bad Moon Rising."

At the driveway, I jumped the ditch, making sure to keep my newly shined boots out of the ice encrusted mud. I dodged a low hanging branch, snagged my jeans on a blackberry briar, leaned against a barbed wire fence.

Dale parked his truck beside an old storm cellar. The engine was off, but he still had his foot on the brakes. Suddenly, the brake lights went dark and his door opened. In front of me was a metal Butler building, nothing special, single door on the right, double garage door on the left. A mercury light shone at the peak in the center. Could have been a body shop, a small engine repair, chain saws sharpened and all that. Pick-ups parked along the hedgerow. Light yellowed the door windows. No one was in sight. Hedge leaves stirred. Coyotes yelped from back in the pits.

42

The garage door started to open. A bright fluorescent light escaped from under it into the gravel parking lot. Dale stopped and looped his hand protectively around Candy's wrist. He angled himself between her and the opening door. They backed up a couple of steps, and then the same guy from Elsie's in the Carhartt jacket stepped out from around the building. Dale swung Candy behind him. I couldn't hear what they were saying. Dale waved, pointed first to the shop then back towards his truck. Carhartt stood dumbly, watching, his hands stuffed in his pockets.

Inside the garage I heard a familiar car start. Nancy's Gremlin drove out. She was driving, cigarette glowing in her lips. She glanced once at Dale and Candy, then gunned the engine and drove right past them onto the dirt road. Instead of right, she turned left away from Highway 7. I hoped Gator had his dome light off. As she hit the dirt, she was close enough to me that I could have taken two steps out of the bushes and rapped on her window. I didn't, hidden instead behind the twisted hedge tree. The backseat of her car was stacked with boxes. Lyle Cuff walked from the garage. He had a pistol in his hand and was tapping it vigorously against his leg.

"What the hell is this?" he said, his voice shrill and agitated. He raised his pistol in Dale's direction.

I squeezed myself from between the fence post and the trees, began to move around the edge of the parking lot, keeping low, sticking to the shadows behind the line of trucks. I didn't have a plan, just a need to see what Lyle and Nancy were up to.

43

Inside the Butler building boxes marked Samsung, Sony, RCA were stacked neatly against the one wall that was visible to me. There were smaller boxes too, the size of camcorders, coffee makers, the works. Lyle was running a regular country electronics shop.

"What the hell is this?" Lyle said again.

"Nothing, Lyle," Dale said, obviously shaken by the pistol.

"Nothing my ass," Lyle walked menacingly towards the two. "Don't give me that shit."

"Weed," Dale said. "I ran out of weed. Thought maybe I could get some more."

Lyle stopped and cocked his head. "Weed. You drove all this way out here in the middle of the goddamn night for pot."

"Yeah," Dale said.

"Who's this?" He pointed at Candy.

"My friend."

"I hope so, dipshit. What's her name?'

"Candy," she said.

"Can . . . dee," Lyle said. "And you want pot?"

They both nodded.

"And you think for some goddamn reason you can drive out to my place anytime you want and expect me to sell you a joint."

"No. That's not it," Dale said. "I didn't think you'd mind."

"Not mind?" Lyle glanced at Carhartt. "Kid thinks we got nothing else to do but wait on his sorry ass."

Lyle couldn't keep his hands steady. If not shaking and pointing his pistol, he was flinging his free hand around like he was shooing flies.

"Lyle," Dale said, "I didn't think. I didn't know you were busy."

"Busy," Lyle's voice rose an octave. "You don't know shit."

"We'll just go."

Dale stepped back, but Lyle pushed forward.

"You'll go when I say go."

"We'll just go," Dale repeated.

"Like hell."

"We didn't see anything," Dale said.

"See what?" Lyle twisted his head on his skinny neck. "What the hell is that supposed to mean? See what?"

"We'll just go."

Lyle swung his pistol against Dale's nose. Dale cried out in pain and dropped to the ground. Candy screamed and turned to run. Carhartt lunged in front of her and shoved her to the ground. Ass flat. Her scream dissolved into tears.

"You go when I say go."

"Bring these two inside," Lyle said. "Nobody goes nowhere. Nobody goes nowhere until I say so."

Lyle Cuff had flipped. Smacking Dale might just be the beginning. I stayed put. My knees weak. I didn't see what I could have done, it all happened so fast. I hid in the shadows as best I could. Lyle was hopped up. Dale Reynolds was not a threat. His dad was Lyle's friend. Probably his business partner.

I edged back the way I'd come, stopping before I got to the gate and crept under the barbed wire fence.

My jacket snagged on a barb. I should have just eased forward until it came free. But I pulled harder. The wire bent with my weight and then snapped forward. I may as well have tossed a lit firecracker. Lyle swung around on his heel and fired at the noise. The bullet rattled high in the trees. I leapt backwards to my feet and ran. Tree branches smacking me in the face, briars trying to pull me down. I ducked blindly in the direction of Gator's car, but I'd cut too far to the south. I stumbled out onto the tracks several yards away from where we'd parked. I fell on the scree, left hand slamming into the iron rail. The car door swung open and Angel ran down the tracks to my side.

"We got to go," I said. "We got to go."

Gator started his engine, back wheels sliding toward the ditch. Angel shoved me into the seat and then jumped in on top of me. Two shadows moved into the clearing behind us. "Stop or I'll shoot your ass," Lyle's pitched voice rang out. He fired the gun into the air. Gator floored the gas pedal and we fishtailed out of the cinder turn-around towards Highway 7. A quarter mile down the road, after Angel and I had pried ourselves out of the tangle of arms and legs, we saw a set of truck headlights ahead of us. I was breathing heavy, heart thumping.

"Shit," Gator said. He down shifted into third, swinging his car almost into the ditch on the right. Doyle Martin's tow truck passed us on the left, a few inches of clearance. He was towing a '57 Chevy.

"What in the hell is going on?" Gator shouted over the engine noise.

I told them.

44

Rita rolled her window down. The November air rushed into the backseat, swirled across the back window, and then ran up the driver's side. In a few seconds I was chilled. She stuck her head through the opening, her hair blowing back from her face, earrings against her skin.

"Go back," she said, dragging her head back inside. "I can't leave Candy." She rolled the window back into place.

I couldn't believe what I was hearing. "Lyle shot at us."

Anger flashed in Rita's eyes. I was immediately sorry I'd said anything. She stared at me hard like I was the enemy. "That's why. He's nuts. He's got my cousin."

"Cuff wouldn't hurt her," Gator said.

"He smashed Dale in the head with a damn gun," she snapped.

I couldn't argue with her. I'd seen what Lyle could do.

"What can we do?" he said.

"Something, Gator. Not just drive away," Rita said.

"He'll calm down. Not even Lyle Cuff wants to go to jail."

"That's what he's trying to avoid," I said, some of what I'd seen suddenly making sense.

Rita bore down on me with her eyes. "What's that mean?"

"The boxes. TVs. Booze. Nancy's car full. More stacked in the building." Then I remembered. My house. Lyle's stolen shit. Cigarettes. Cases of whiskey.

The furrow in Rita's brow deepened. "Crap."

"Yeah," I said.

Angel lowered his head. He rested his cast against Rita's leg.

"Hijackers," I said.

"What the hell are you talking about?" Gator said.

Rita threw herself back in the seat. "At work, those others you said were inside, I think they drive trucks for Monroe. They were twisted about something yesterday."

"You heard them?" Angel asked.

"No. Just the way they were talking. All heated. Then tonight, another truck."

"That could have been anything. Girlfriend problems. Football," Gator said. "It doesn't mean they're hijackers."

Rita nodded her head. "I wouldn't have thought more about it. They had the trucking docket out. The shift schedule."

"So what? No one has been hijacking crates of chickens."

"I don't know. They were looking over their shoulders. Whispering."

"Jesus," Gator said under his breath.

Rita snapped, "Lyle did it. Had to be. No wonder he's half crazy. This time they put the truck driver in the hospital."

Angel rubbed the tops of his thighs. "We can't leave Candy and Dale with those fools."

Rita nodded.

The GTO rumbled down the dirt road toward Highway 7.

"Too dangerous to go back. We have to do something else," I said.

Angel agreed, "Call the police."

None of us trusted the police. By that I mean none of us trusted Sheriff Douglas. Lyle's buddy. "Douglas might be in on the whole thing," Rita said. "We know he's in on the drugs."

"Mr. Reynolds?" I asked.

Gator slowed the car as we came up to the stop sign at the highway. "Dale's in a world of pain," he said.

"His dad is involved. Maybe a little. Maybe a lot."

"How far to Willy's?" Rita asked.

Gator leaned forward to get a better look at the road. "Right over that rise."

"Go," she said. "I'll make the call."

"Call who?" I asked.

"I'm thinking," she said.

45

The lights above the pumps were lit, but the store itself was dimmed to gray. Obviously closed. "Willy's never closes," Gator said as we slowed into the parking lot.

Out back, the parking lot ran for a hundred yards to where it met a fenced pasture. A couple of rigs were sitting quietly with their running lights on. Gator drove in under the first canopy and shut down the motor. Two Ford Fairlanes had nosed up to the front door. Plastic crime tape was stretched like a fence around the set of diesel pumps farthest from the door. Inside the store I could see two men leaning on the counter. In the gray light of the refrigerator cases, a bright FBI stencil shone from the back of one of the men.

"Damn," Angel said. "Big guns."

"Hijacking crosses state lines," I said.

Rita glanced my way. "We don't have to worry about Douglas now."

Angel grabbed his door handle. "Let's get this over with."

Gator let out a sigh. "You sure?"

"Shit's going to hit the fan," Angel said.

"You go," I said. "I can't."

They all looked at me.

"Nancy," I said, my face in my hands. "I can't just turn her in."

No one said anything.

"Like some kind of Hitler Youth turning in my mother."

"Jesus," Angel said. "I didn't think."

"So, what do we do?" Gator asked.

From my window, the highway disappeared into the darkness toward Cliggett City. My friends were in trouble. Lyle and Nancy were to blame. Responsibility. Guilt.

Rita yanked her purse from the floor. "Fuck you all. Candy's my cousin."

Gator opened the driver's door and heaved himself out of the front seat. "We go, Danny. No one expects you to come in."

I opened my door and stepped outside. Fed up with it all.

46

Standing beside the diesel pumps, I shivered in the cold. The jacket I thought had been my dad's was left hanging from Lyle's barbed wire fence. I stuck my hands deep in my pockets, hunched my shoulders against the wind.

"Here," Angel took off his letter jacket and tossed it to me. "You keep this. You earned it whether Coach agrees or not. I'll steal another."

"No, man," I said. Angel raised his hand to silence me.

A tear ran out of my left eye. I wiped it away before anyone could see. As we followed Rita past the fried chicken sign, Angel rested his hand on my shoulder. We stood in front of the glass door staring at our reflection. It was pushed away by an FBI agent as he opened the door. I had this feeling nothing would ever be the same.

O mother,
even in the same house
you live so far away

47

For the next few days, I slept on Rita's couch while Cliggett City buzzed with noise about the arrest of Lyle Cuff. Nancy was picked up at Elsie's the next afternoon. Mr. Reynolds would represent them all in court. I still suspected he'd been more than legal counsel with the pot farm. So far, no one talked marijuana, just trucks, stolen electronics, whiskey.

Rita worked at Monroe's. Candy helped her mother clean houses. I watched old movies on AMC. I hadn't been to school. Angel said to stay low until the dust settled. He and Gator had driven over to Tomato Road to pick up my clothes. They said the house had been turned upside down. Every kitchen cabinet open. Every dresser. The couch cushions. Mattresses flipped. No sign of Merle.

Rita suggested I seek emancipation. I asked her if I needed Abraham Lincoln for that.

She sighed. I let it drop. But the idea gave me hope. On the third day I decided to find Merle. So, I left Rita's and walked across town. I was picked up by the police outside of Beth's house just before jumping the barbed wire. In hindsight I shouldn't have worn Angel's letter jacket. Shouldn't have crossed a neighborhood like Nottingham. Shouldn't have. Shouldn't have.

164

But I did. The Cliggett City cops found me standing in front of Beth's. Two cops for one dumb kid.

When they put me in the patrol car, hand on my head, I wasn't handcuffed, wasn't searched. They were polite, happy, eager to finally be involved in Cliggett City's crime wave. I was a celebrity.

Not a curtain breathed
on any of Beth's windows.
No one home.
Across the fields,
the roof of my house
clipped the horizon.
Merle waited in the barn,
rolling a dead
mouse in the dirt.

48

A man named Bill Brennan met us at the station. He introduced himself as my social worker. My case worker, he called it. I realized that I knew his son from biology class. Yeah. That class. Bill didn't bring biology up, so I didn't either.

We shook hands. Bill asked if I was hungry. I was always hungry. He told the cops we were going to lunch. They handed him paperwork to sign. And we left through the front door, rather than through a window.

At the Dairy Mary we took a booth in back. Bill ordered a cheeseburger and fries. I ordered the same.

"Isn't that Angel Chavez's letter jacket?" He said.

"You know Angel?" I said.

"I know all you guys in one way or another." That must have been an inside joke. He laughed. I smiled.

"My son is in the school band. Drummer. I never miss a game."

I remembered Tony Brennan, long haired kid with an earring.

Bill stirred his coffee. Pushed the cup under his moustache and took a sip. His eyes never left me. Like they were searching my face for a zit, a crack in my armor.

"You've been through a lot lately."

I stabbed a straw into my Coke. Didn't answer.

"How did you get me out?"

"The station?"

"Yeah."

Bill set his cup down in front of him. "You're not charged with anything, Danny. As far as anyone knows, you haven't done anything wrong." Bill smiled. "Have you?"

"No hijacking," I said.

Bill laughed. The waitress brought two cheeseburger baskets to our table. We sat back so she could slide them in front of us. Bill picked up his coffee. "Thanks kiddo," he said.

"Could I get ketchup?" I asked.

She pointed to the plastic ketchup bottle next to the napkins.

"Thanks," I said.

"No problem, Danny," she said.

After she walked away, Bill asked if I knew everybody in town. I shrugged. "Don't know who she is," I said.

"You're famous."

"Bull."

Bill took the ketchup bottle from my hand and squirted a red lake on his plate. It drained on the unlevel table into the shape of Lake Michigan. A pond for himself.

49

Dale and Candy sat in the hallway of the County Court Center with Rita. They would eventually be called as witnesses against Lyle Cuff. But that's not why they were here today. Today was about me. I was with the judge and Bill Brennan. I'd been classified as "a child in need of care." My first reaction to that was "Yeah, no shit." My second reaction, as Bill explained it to me, was, "Damn. I'm going to kid jail."

It was true. Nothing would ever be the same.

Bill explained in a calm voice that I hadn't done anything wrong. In fact, the judge thought highly of me.

I said, "OK, then let me go. I've been taking care of myself since I started high school."

Bill further explained that since I wasn't eighteen, I was to become a ward of the state. That meant the state of Kansas was now my mother and father.

"Some parents," I'd answered him sarcastically. Buffalo and meadowlarks, a real "Home on the Range." Bill thought that was funny and he started to laugh.

The judge was a young guy. That surprised me. I thought all judges were white-haired and wise looking. Judge Dyson looked like a bartender. Black hair, short goatee. Bouncer arms. Shirt unbuttoned at the collar. His eyes never left me. I was to be placed at Spencer House, whatever the hell that was. Some youth home up by Topeka. Bill would transport me there later today. Transport me. Like I was some kind of . . . yeah, box of crackers.

At Lyle's arraignment, he discovered that we were witnesses for the prosecution, and he'd blown a gasket. Must have been the strain of living without alcohol and cocaine, he threatened to kill us all. Me twice. At that point I was still at Rita's. I suggested to Bill that she could be my guardian. One look at Rita's long legs, and Bill laughed. Keep dreaming, kid, he said. All of Cliggett City followed the news—even Franky's mother had come to see me. She didn't bring Franky. She said he'd be agitated by all the excitement. Hell, I was agitated. Welcome to the club. Bill told me that she'd considered letting me stay with them until Lyle had threatened to kill me twice. I asked him if killing me once would have kept me in her foster plans. Bill laughed. Said that he liked my sense of irony. Either way, my options were limited. Lyle and his thugs were in County. Their prospects dim. Nancy would fare better when she went to rehab since she hadn't hijacked any trucks, but she had aided and abetted, the judge said. Sheriff Douglas would skate. An investigation was launched. But so far, his only crime was stupidity. I knew better.

When I stepped out into the hall with Bill and a pocketful of Judge Dyson's best wishes, the brothers had arrived. They'd finally gotten the green food coloring from under their fingernails. The blame for the green chickens had yet to fall on anyone's shoulders. I didn't much give a shit at this point. High school pranks were chump change compared to Spencer House, the judicial system, a convict mother.

The brothers gave me a hug, sliding a can of Skoal into my back pocket. I didn't even chew. Dale smiled and said he'd write. "Cool," I said. Rita and Candy kissed me on the cheek.

"We will feed your dog," Candy said.

"Cat," I said.

"She knows." Rita said. "Maybe he comes to my house."

Good-bye, Merle, I said to myself. I'd lost him forever to Rita.

50

The elevator door opened, Gator and Angel came in and handed me a plastic bag of clothes. Angel said I'd be back in no time.

"You're like twelve, right? Only six more years, Scud Boy."

"Yeah. I'm twelve." We both laughed.

Gator rubbed his boobs on me. "Something to remember me by."

I left with Bill before the duck got out of my throat again. I didn't want things to end on a quacking sob note.

Bill said I had to sit in back and buckle up.

"More laws," I said.

He said, "Affirmative buddy."

We drove north out of town past the Dairy Mary. I caught the smell of greasy cheeseburgers and fries. Just past the road to the chicken factory, we flew by the sign that said *Welcome to Cliggett City—Chicken Capital of Kansas.*

SPENCER HOUSE

51

Sparks the Arsonist spit on the steel security screen, pressed it with his thumb until he squeezed saliva through into the cold wind. He spooked me. I'd wake in the middle of the night and he'd be standing at his window, not smoking, not playing with himself, just watching the lights glowing on the horizon. Steel screens don't look like bars. But they work just as well.

Tonight, Robert the floor counselor had been doing bed checks. I heard him stop at Sparks's room.

"Trouble sleeping?" Robert asked, opening the door.

"I'm freeing my boogers," Sparks said.

"You're what?"

"I'm pushing them out through the holes in the screen."

"That's gross, man."

Sparks shrugged. "Not as gross as this place."

Robert clicked the off/on switch on his flashlight. A small circle of light bounced off the floor, flashed across the bare walls, the single dresser.

Sparks faced him.

"Let me out," he said.

"Sure," Robert replied, clicking the flashlight.

"I'm ready to go."

I waited for Sparks's punch line. Silence filled the air between the two of them.

Sparks pointed to the horizon of lights. "Unlock it," he said.

"The window? No way."

"The door. Just unlock it."

Robert set his flashlight on the desk. "You know I can't let you out."

"You've got a key card. I'm ready."

The thing that got me about Sparks was his lack of emotion, flat line on the Richter scale. Robert scratched his nose.

"Why do you think I should let you out?" Robert asked, folding his arms across his chest.

"I've had enough of this place," Sparks said.

Robert laughed softly, "Can't let you out, Sparks. You know that. Go back to sleep. It's the middle of the night."

Sparks sighed, sat on his bed.

Robert closed his door. He looked through the window. Then headed back to the floor office.

"Weird little guy," he said to himself.

52

I took my hairbrush and wrapped a length of wire around the handle. Looped it through the hole on the end of the brush so that about ten inches stuck out straight like a small sword. Then I unraveled some toilet paper out of my pocket, wrapped a twist around the wire.

I checked my door window once more for Robert's flashlight. When I didn't see it bobbing on room checks, I slipped a cigarette from the groove behind my door jamb. I never smoked before Spencer, but it's the only extra-curricular activity available. Kind of a game, finding cigarettes, trading them, not getting caught. A sport. Holding the brush by its bristles, I pushed the wire into the electric outlet. Electricity ran up the wire and ignited the toilet paper. I bent to light the cigarette. I laid the glowing paper on my windowsill and smashed it out with my fist. I loved the way the paper crinkled red and alive like the scales of a dragon. When I pulverized them, they scattered like people, here one moment, then gone, sucked through the open window. Cold nights draw fast.

nights cold nights
smoke escaping
through a screen

53

I have been locked up a few weeks, but I already know what's important at Spencer House. What you can't get. Matches and cigarettes and Coca Cola. I guess that's true everywhere. We always want what we can't get—gold, diamonds, love. Matches are forbidden, more forbidden than cigarettes. Cigarettes are valuable, and I know how to get them. I've got to write this story of mine, because if I don't, then I won't get cigarettes. Two days ago, I gave two for a St. Louis Cardinals ball cap. It was brand-ass new. The kid who owned it was a nicotine junkie. He'd probably stolen the hat from some other slob.

The real problem is matches. We've got a few guys at Spencer who get off on burning shit down—you know, barns, houses, trucks, churches. So, matches are serious. You get caught with them and it's like the electric chair. The staff takes away all your privileges and throws you in isolation for twenty-four hours. That's not worth it to me.

I'm not an arsonist. I'm not any kind of criminal really. I've stolen, but only little shit. And I've never been caught. Well, except for the car. Although, I didn't really steal it. Just borrowed. And I was only an accessory. Dale stole the car. Rita drove. Muff point. I mean, moot point. My crimes aren't why I'm here. It's more like I'm here for my own good. That's what the judge said. Personally, I think he ought to spend one night on the floor or eat the food or watch TV with all these weird dicksticks, rubbing their crotches, farting cumulus clouds. Then let him tell me Spencer House is for my own good and maybe I'll believe him.

I've got an angle to make life better, and that is to get out, but first I need cigarettes, like, for power. Second, this journal is my job. Oh, it's not like my counselor is paying me off in Camels. No, that wouldn't work with Anne. She's too straight. It's just that she leaves me alone in her office, so I can "compose" my thoughts. Compose is her word. She has this idea that if I write everything out, then the "trauma," her word again, of being abandoned will work its way out of my system. Anne said, talk to the paper. But no cussing. Use higher level vocabulary. Hell, I can't even think without profanity so I'm just leaving out the F-bomb . . . almost. I'm already a lost cause. Nancy made certain of that. The first word I ever said was bitch.

Anne keeps her Marlboros in her purse, her purse under her desk, her desk locked in her first-floor office, and I steal them. Every time we meet. Just before I push the button on my ball point pen. Click.

54

The door opened, but not before the knob rattled. That was typical of Anne. It's like her signal. She turns, pauses, then opens the door. This time she was talking to one of the other counselors. I had my feet tucked under the chair and my head leaned back while I counted the ceiling tiles. I'd memorized them. I also knew the schedules of staff, cooks, janitors, painters. I knew when the food truck delivered canned vegetables, and when the mail carrier brought the mail. The one thing I couldn't be sure of was when the Sheriff was going to come by. He was like a storm, rumbling out of nowhere in his big black and white. And when they brought in new kids, dirt-faced, stinking of fear, and don't-give-a-shit smirks, that could be any time. Effing up doesn't keep a schedule.

Anne slipped an armload of manila folders onto the desk. They contained personal crap about the guys I shared the floor with. You know, sicko stuff like who wets the bed, and who spanks his monkey more than twice a day. Who bonked his sister? Who got beat by his dad? It's all in a folder.

Anne tapped me on the forehead with her finger. *Thunk. Thunk.*

"How's the story coming?"

I could smell her perfume. It was light, not like flowers or fruit, but an incense that floats right out of her skin. "OK," I said, sitting up straighter in my chair. Not because I recognized her as any kind of authority like a cop or a principal, but because she was a woman. One afternoon after looking over my story, Anne said my statements about women weren't always respectful. That confused me. She said that girls, women, didn't like being objectified. My face went blank. Later, I went through the story and crossed out a lot of boob references that I thought were funny. I didn't see how this would help the world much unless I could start crossing out half of what I heard every day. Jesus, that would take Carrie Nation.

Anne sat down on the front of her desk after dumping her jacket in her chair. She brushed her brown hair back from her face and smiled.

"Doing any better with Chucky?" she asked. Chucky—this asshole who'd been giving me crap for the past week. He'd just arrived from Kansas City, and sticking his face into my face was his main hobby. It was a big-dog thing Chucky learned through osmosis from his father. Chucky had one gear, low and slow, like a bulldozer.

"Not really," I answered. "One of these days someone's going to wrap a pool cue around his head." I got a buzz out of talking tough to Anne.

She sighed and shook her head. "That's a quick solution that will get us nowhere, Danny."

Us. A bond.

But I knew that. I was Spencer's Mahatma Gandhi. Nonviolent, you know. Still, Gandhi or not, I liked messing with Anne. I could tell she was upset because her cheeks flushed. Anne hadn't been out of college too long. She said Spencer was her first counseling job. She really wanted to help me out, to change the world one asshole at a time. So, I said, "Yeah. I know. Beating Chucky Swallow with a cue stick won't help us find world peace."

She laughed. Like maybe she'd given me some new reason not to smash his face into pizza.

Today was torture. No different than the last session. I couldn't take my eyes off her legs. They were perfect. I wanted to lick her kneecaps. OK, so much for Gandhi, I was objectifying again.

"Did you get a lot done?" She flipped the pages of my notebook.

"I think so."

When you don't see girls regularly, well, the ones you do see are goddesses. Every time Anne bent over, I tried to look down her blouse. I couldn't help myself. I was a child in need of care. Still, part of me hated the fact that I was having to use Anne, playing her for cigarettes. But I didn't see where I had much choice if I wanted to get out of Spencer.

"Anne." She smiled and looked at me expectantly. "Why don't you just adopt me?"

She laughed. "You're hopeless, Danny." She turned around and walked behind her desk. I couldn't believe the crap I said to her, I used to be shy, but recent events had pissed the shyness right out of me.

"I could shovel snow. Mow grass."

"What do you think you learned today?" She leaned forward over her desk to prove that her question was important. I tried not to stare down her blouse, but I had to. The monkey made me.

"I learned that I'm not Gandhi."

55

Immediate compliance. That's one thing I never learned. The words popped into my head like a gunshot. Must have heard it somewhere, like in school. Principal's office. Or else at group. What I learned was that I can't do immediate compliance. Even from Coach. If someone says, "Do something Prego," I've got to wait, roll it over in my brain like dice. Then, maybe I do, maybe I don't. That's one way I'm like these jerks at Spencer. At least, I know the word—compliance.

Chucky Swallow was my enemy on the floor. He got in my shit every time I showered, took a piss, played pool, sat in a vinyl chair. From my doorway, I could watch him in his room dunking a wadded sock ball in a wire hoop he'd bent out of a coat hanger. He was working up a sweat, huffing and puffing flooding the hallway, even above the radios and CD players that were blaring. This was one of the better times at Spencer—just before lights out—after we'd cleaned up, brushed our teeth, drained the weasel, and scrubbed our little faces. It meant we were room-bound, and nobody could mess with us. We had time then for our thoughts—to read or listen to music or stare down the hall, plan to run. Me, I read and wrote in my notebook. Anne kept me loaded with books. Used college texts. I'd complained that the

Spencer library was perfect for third graders. I'd read every comic book in the bookcase. I'd even read parts of the World Book Encyclopedia, an incomplete set. Missing the S volume. I'd picked up the A book. Someone had colored in it with crayon. Purple penises. Anne brought me Gandhi, a bit of Thoreau, although he was tough as hell. I understood about every third word.

We weren't allowed to own much on the floor. I mean personal stuff. Level Ones weren't allowed shit until they'd proven to the staff that they could follow the rules. I could. I moved through the levels like shit through a goose. That's Coach Amber's line. I was up to Level Three which meant I could stay up until midnight and watch TV. I could also wear my own clothes, not just the Spencer logo T-shirts, jeans, and black Converse low tops. I had my own jeans, a Cliggett City Football hoodie, boots, and Angel's letter jacket. That was pretty much it. We were all equally peasants. More bonding.

Chucky Swallow, a Level Two, owns his sock ball and wire basket. That's it. No words, no music, no brains, all asshole, and sock. He works himself crazy, banging and slamming into his walls—bouncing, faking, jumping, and fading. That way when the lights go black, he can spank his monkey and fall asleep. Chucky hates the darkness. Most do, but Chucky most of all. He has bad dreams every night. I know because I can hear him crying, shouting into his pillow. Everybody hears him because few can sleep nights at Spencer. We lay awake in the darkness and take naps all day.

At first, I felt sorry for Chucky, before he got in my face. He had nothing. Fear. Resentment. Confusion. His abuse started when I put on Angel's letter jacket. Big dick, he called me. I said, yes. "Takes one to know one." Chucky didn't get it. So, I let him become a part of my plan. When I reach Level Four, I get unsupervised time off the campus. I can walk out into a wheatfield and look at the clouds. I can walk down to the Gas Stop. Buy a Coke.

56

I pulled the blankets over my head and shut out the sounds of the floor. Radios were popping on and the showers were sizzling hot for the first five minutes of the morning. Just as sure as sunshine, the bickering began, a religion at Spencer. It didn't matter over what—could be a towel or shampoo or a place in line by the door, waiting too long for breakfast. It didn't matter, conflict was created out of nothing.

Good morning, assholes, I thought before pulling the pillow over my ears. My window, open from the night's cigarette, chilled the room like the coldest beer in town. I closed my eyes again, but I couldn't see Cliggett City—not my house—not the people. Finally, a picture of Franky formed in my mind. I smiled, then Gator slipped in and Coach Amber. Then Beth Wilkins. She smiled.

"When?" she asked.

I knew what she meant, but I didn't have the "when" figured out yet. "Soon," I said aloud. "Soon as I have a plan," which was partly true because I did have a plan beginning—a plan to run, go AWOL.

The door to my room swung open and banged against the wall. A flood of noise from the hallway swept Beth aside. I tossed back the covers, expecting to see the day staff rousting me from bed, but instead, Swallow stood in the doorway with a towel around his waist and little headlights gleaming from his eyes.

"Get out!" I said.

He studied the hallway, and stepped deeper into my room, turned his butt towards me and cut a long fart. "Eat that for breakfast, jerk off!" Then he strutted out, flapping his towel, laughing like an idiot.

57

"How about I take this wire and cut up your face?"
First words after sausage links and dried eggs.

It was Sparks. He had a clothes hanger wrapped around his wrist. He shook it menacingly at Swallow.

Yes, I thought. *Slice the bastard into chicken livers.*

Chucky smiled, cold like a Chevy grill. Never lifting his eyes from Sparks, he grabbed the pool cue that was leaning against the table. He gripped the stick like a cudgel.

I had this impulse to palm the eight ball and bounce it off the back of Chucky's head.

"You nothing, boy," Sparks sneered and began to circle.

"Just try, and I show you what nothing do." He popped the cue against the flat of his hand.

Again, Chucky Swallow smacked the palm of his hand. Sparks's eyes darted around the game room. I sat up to see if any of the staff were in the hallway, and as far as I could tell they were still in the laundry room with Drew. He'd just dried a box of crayons in the dryer to see what color they'd melt into. Now, he was scraping off the sides of the dryer with a plastic spatula.

Nobody wanted to step in between Sparks and Chucky. They were the craziest on the floor. The difference was that Sparks was a firebug, not a fighter. Chucky would shred him like a tortilla. None of the residents gave a shit. They lapped up fights, a diversion from boredom. They flocked like crows around a dead armadillo.

The realization that he was going to get his head knocked off sunk into Sparks's kerosene-soaked brain. He licked his lips, glanced nervously around the room. When he turned to edge out the door, I saw fear. Chucky saw it, too.

"Sit your ass!" Chucky barked. He kicked Sparks the desk chair. Sparks flinched, the pool cue about to crack the bridge of his skull.

"Watch it," I said. "He's just a little kid."

Chucky swung the pool cue and caught me on the arm, smacking the bone right above the elbow. Pain shot up my arm and into the base of my brain. I tumbled against the pool table, scattering the balls and flipping the triangle over. He swung again. Whacked my shoulder. I lunged over the side of the table and picked up the thirteen ball. I threw as hard as I could and missed Chucky's throat by an inch. Fat Larry, the daytime floor counselor, opened the stairway door and the ball caught him on the shoulder. He dropped like a heavy book, the T encyclopedia of trouble.

In seconds, the staff was all over us. I got pushed into a corner by the television by Randy, Robert's brother. Blake Wilson yanked the pool cue out of Chucky's hand and shoved him into the staff office. Fighting on the floor meant instant demotion. Both of us could get busted to Level One. Fighters cooled their anger in isolation. If they were good boys, compliant, and explained to the counselor's satisfaction that they understood the consequences of fighting, they'd be released back into gen pop. A problem was that we only had one Isolation Room per floor.

I explained that I'd thrown the thirteen ball at Chucky's brain, but it was so small that I'd missed. That's why Fat Larry had been hit. Sparks backed me up. Still, it was a fight. Weapons were devised from ordinary game room toys and used to do physical harm. I was guilty. Sent to my room with the promise that I wouldn't leave. The staff gathered up my personal possessions in a file box and left me to think about my behavior while sitting on my bed.

Chucky got locked up. "Effin' unfair," he said, so pissed that I thought his eyes were going to pop out of his skull. I scratched my nose with my middle finger as he was being led away. Chucky had a juvenile record for drugs, theft. I was just labeled as a child in need. They weighed differently in Spencer's books. Chucky was trouble. I was a victim. Chucky got real lock-up. I earned room detention. Sparks stood by me. He knew I'd saved his skinny ass.

That night, after Chucky got tired of kicking the inside of the metal door, Sparks slipped into my room. His hair was washed, combed back above his widow's peak. His eyes were sad, sparkled like fire going out. He asked if I wanted him to beat me off.

58

Two cigarettes late in the night. One I sucked on slowly, letting the smoke drift up below the window and out of the screen into the open sky. The other sat on the windowsill, ready for when the first was about to go out. I'd light it off the butt of the first. I was allowing myself two cigarettes. A celebration for not getting busted down. One day in room detention. Only leaving to pee and eat. Chucky was released to his room, but he tapped my window and flipped me off as he was escorted to his room.

Robert busted him back to isolation. I had nearly knocked Fat Larry senseless just as he stepped onto the floor with a blob of melted crayons in his hand. (PS—the color was purple and green.)

I liked Larry, the spitting image of Meatloaf. He knew it, lip-synched "Paradise by the Dashboard Lights" on Valentine's Day.

Now, the Superintendent talked about assault. Fat Larry had the bruise to prove it, but in my favor, he called bullshit. Danny threw the ball in self-defense, not at me. Anne stood beside him. I had allies.

Later than usual, maybe four or five in the morning. A delivery truck churned up the gravel drive and swung around behind the building to the kitchen service door. That's where we took out the trash. Right beside the sink where Level Threes washed the dishes.

59

I explained the fight to Anne. She believed me. She rubbed her temples like she was unwinding a clock. She was wearing a lot of makeup today, more blush than usual and her eyeliner was darker. Most guys my age don't notice this kind of stuff, but makeup was always a clue to Nancy's behavior. Too much meant she felt bad and was trying to cover up. No makeup meant she felt terrible and had quit caring. All the little in-betweens were significant. Her mood sought a balance between caked-on base layer and raw skin. I played them like a linebacker reading an offensive formation, always ready to adjust.

My story didn't help Anne's mood. I guessed she was having boyfriend problems. None of my business. She sighed after a few moments of silence and told me that Larry was the right dude to accidentally hit with a pool ball. A no grudge kind of guy.

She tapped out a Marlboro onto her desk.

"Danny, fights between the boys on the floor happen all the time. The staff writes them up and the consequences usually stop at Spencer . . ." she paused and picked at a cuticle. "But when a staff member gets involved, especially when a weapon is used . . ."

"A thirteen ball," I said.

She laughed.

"It could involve the law. That means the courts, and it gets out of Spencer's hands."

"What are you saying?"

"I'm saying you could have gone to court on criminal charges. Got shipped to a lock-up facility. You could . . ."

"This is a lock-up facility," I said.

She lit her Marlboro and then put the pack in the cabinet behind her desk. My eyes widened when I saw the carton on the shelf, a whole carton, barely opened, crisp and mostly untouched. Smoking in the building, even for staff, was against the rules.

Anne was distracted, not thinking clearly. She'd never shown me her stash before, never pulled a cigarette out of anywhere except her purse. I almost asked.

"Yes. Somewhat," she said. "Spencer doesn't compare to some of the state facilities. We don't want you to end up at State School for one screw up."

Nice plain name for a prison. Every kid on the floor knew about State School. Sliding bars and fenced yard with the curling razor wire. State was serious, a level beyond Spencer's metal security screens and unlocked dorm rooms."

She blew a jet of smoke. "We need to get you out of here."

"What's that mean?"

"Probably foster care."

I sucked my lower lip. "What about declaring myself independent? Emancipation. Going back to my house in Cliggett City."

Anne didn't answer. "You've had two people check in with us. A Bob Carl from over by Pittsburg, and a Mrs. Weathers from Cliggett City."

"Weathers?"

"She wrote that she had a special needs boy named . . ."

"Franky," I said.

"Yes. Franky. Mrs. Weathers says you're her son's protector."

"Kids on the bus mess with him."

Anne smiled. "There's more than one Sparks in the world."

She tapped my notebook and left the room. A strong whiff of smoke and perfume hung above my head when she brushed past.

I waited after the door latched before jumping behind her desk and opening the cabinet. I slipped an unopened pack of Marlboro into my pants, gently nudging the remaining packs to the front of the carton. I stuck it in my underwear so they wouldn't slide down my jeans. Guilt. I gave guilt the finger and opened my notebook. Two truths. Both real.

Miss Finch found me in eighth grade. I was sitting by myself in the hallway outside of the cafeteria reading *Catcher in the Rye*. Honestly, I just opened the book. All the kids knew who she was. She taught upstairs with the high school kids. She stood out. Most of our teachers were antiques, aged Victorian women with ankle high black shoes. Miss Finch wore denim jeans and a blue tie-dye on game days. Her hair was long and straight, parted in the middle. She wore a silver POW bracelet and black and white high top tennis shoes. On more formal occasions like parent-teacher conferences, she wore skirts that rose a little above her knees. "You like the book?" she said.

I hadn't seen her walk up, so I was startled. I turned the book over to the cover as if I were reading the title for the first time. "I don't know," I said. "I like baseball."

She knotted her brow. "Baseball?"

"Yeah. I played second base in Little League."

Suddenly, she smiled, her forehead relaxing. "Ah. The catcher."

I was confused.

"Keep reading," she said. "You might find this story more provocative than baseball."

Provocative, I thought. *That's a big word to pull on a random eighth grader.*

"OK," I said. "I will."

Miss Finch creased the top of her brown sack lunch. "We'll talk again," she said, before stepping into the cafeteria.

We did talk again. Often. I chose my spot in the hallway so that I could see who came and went. Sometimes Miss Finch stopped and talked. Sometimes she gave me a wave and a smile. One Tuesday, she said I should stop by her room during tomorrow's lunch. She was starting a brown bag lunch club.

"What's that?" I said.

She smiled. "Bring your lunch and the book you're reading. You'll see."

On Tuesday I didn't have any lunch. It was one of those empty refrigerator mornings on Tomato Road. So, I didn't go. Miss Finch stopped me in the hall on the way to gym class.

"Every Tuesday," she said. She handed me a book of poems called *A Geography of Poets*. "Drop in if you can."

I dropped in and kept dropping in until Miss Finch became Mrs. Meyer a year later, until she moved to someplace out west like San Francisco or Seattle. A place that started with an S and had an ocean. She handed me an empty notebook on our last Tuesday. She said the notebook was a Moleskin, used by the best.

"Fill it up," she said.

The wind blew cold on Tuesday, bitter cold, snow. Little icy flakes rattled against my nylon jacket. My Cliggett City hoodie and letter jacket were still in a cardboard box. I took a deep breath of air, too deep, and coughed at the sharpness of it. I slipped into the shop door and shivered. An overhead furnace blasted the garage and I let the heat penetrate my shirt.

A light glowed in the back room. Someone moved boxes. It had to be the maintenance man.

"Ed!" I yelled down the hallway. I waited, then hollered again.

"Back here, Marvin." Marvin Webb was the Level Three I'd traded places with for the day. He was going to vacuum offices and I was going to sweep the shop. Marvin had traded for one day. It had cost me ten cigarettes, a fortune.

The shop wasn't big, nothing more than a workshop and a garage. Here, everything at Spencer was repaired, patched, or re-created out of junk. Ed was a master at blending two broken nothings into a workable something. His specialties, bunks and desks. Every kid on the floor had a bunk and desk made of plywood, two by fours, and steel bolts. Each piece was painted battleship gray and was heavy enough to be impossible to throw against the wall.

Level Threes bartered jobs, so Ed wasn't surprised to see me instead of Marvin. He gave me a long-handled broom and a dustpan, then he returned to the work bench where he was gluing a gray board to a brown board. He had them pressed together with wood clamps. No matter what angle, I couldn't tell what he was making. I was certain that at one point it would turn into a desk or a bed.

On the far wall was a brown cabinet. It was always closed, but usually unlocked. That was the gamble I had taken—that the cabinet would be unlocked, and that Ed would have to take a piss. Marvin said that Ed pissed about every five minutes. The cabinet was full of keys, each one labeled and hanging on a brass hook.

If I found a key
that opened the secrets
that you hid in your closet,
I'd keep it protected
once I'd unlocked
the door.

Of course, I'd ask
permission, for the
remainder of my life
to be let in, like now
I ask
again and again
and again and
again.

61

The key dangled on a string from my bird finger. Something I'd learned at home. In the game room light, it glowed with the slight bluish hue of the TV. Sparks's face was a light bulb, wide and vivid with hope.

"That's the key to where?" He gulped.

"Shhh." I pressed a finger to my lips. "You heard me. The south door. Our ticket out."

Sparks touched the key. He slid it through his fingers like it was a weapon, a match, a flame. "You going to use it?"

I peered over Sparks's shoulder into the darkness where a couch was pushed against the wall, turned backwards so that the seat was flush to the plaster. It creaked as Chucky Swallow lifted himself on his shoulder, straining to hear without being seen.

"Yes." I whispered loud enough to be heard. "The ticket out."

"When?" Sparks leaned forward in his seat, oblivious to the rest of the floor.

"Soon—before they figure I swiped it."

"From where?" He blurted.

"My business." That much I didn't want Chucky to know. I placed the key in Sparks's hand.

"Need you to keep it for me. Until I ask for it."

Sparks jerked his hand back. "No way, man. I'll get busted."

"Take it."

I pushed the key back into his hands along with half a pack of Marlboros.

I could see Chucky peeking from under the arm rest.

"Staff use cards."

"Shh!" I warned him. "South door stairwell leads straight outside. No one uses it anymore. No keycard."

Sparks grinned.

"South door is the best way out at night. Staff can't see it from the office. It's my chance to get out before Christmas." I paused to let it sink in. "You can come too."

Sparks shook his head. "No way. I can't. I go home after Christmas. A foster home in my town. I can even go back to my old school."

A pang of jealousy ripped through me. To go home, back with Gator and Angel and Rita. I shook the thought off like a dog does rain. A foster home in Cliggett City was too much to wish for.

"Hide the key then. Two days tops."

"Why me?" Sparks asked.

"I'm in the radar big time. Fat Larry thing." It was a lie.

Sparks stuffed the key in the cigarette package and shoved them both into his pants. He nodded and turned back to watch *Gilligan's Island*. When I stood up, Chucky slumped like he was asleep. What a shitty fake. I smiled as I walked out into the green hallway.

62

The window wasn't high. It was just above the sink—the large stainless steel sink where all the Spencer dishes were rinsed before dumping them in the dishwasher. It had cost another ten Marlboros to trade jobs. Who sets these prices? The kitchen kid wasn't a smoker, so he wasn't hurting like an addict. The lure of wealth was too great.

> *Food swirls in the sink.*
> *When the drain trap is full,*
> *the rinse hose slaps*
> *white bowls to a shine.*
> *Wet chunks of potato*
> *sink into the trash,*
> *the old hope dead,*
> *the new shines*
> *like stainless steel.*

The dishes were stacked in three big dishwashers, just like the kind used in homes. Nothing commercial, nothing complicated. I took my time, playing with the water, thinking.

Chucky knew the best time to run was when the boys were in the game room and the staff was kicked back in the office letting their pork chops settle. That's right, pork chops. I mean it was Christmas Eve, and that's the meal, Christmas pork chops. Lumpy mashed potatoes, thin gravy, and skinny chops, but what the hell, it was better than corn dogs.

63

As expected, Chucky had swiped the key from Sparks yesterday, and I knew he'd leave one of the two days before Christmas. He wanted to be home. He was pissed because he hadn't earned a pass. The fight with me had grounded his ass. Chucky pretended like it was a big deal to go home, but I knew he didn't have anywhere to go. The floor was half-full, and staff was reduced. Staff members were hustling each other for the day off. Anne, too. She'd cut our last session short because of a Christmas party at some guy's house. Gave me ten minutes in her office to write and told me we'd talk about something important after the holiday. Pool ball episode, court time, getting shipped, what else? I left her cigarettes alone today. Had enough anyway. However, just before she came in, I saw a letter from Pullet County Social Services. It had to be about me, since I was Spencer's only kid from that part of the state. I slipped it in my pants. Then I walked to the kitchen to eat and wash dishes and wait. Chucky was due. The early darkness was already sitting on the trees. In a few minutes it would climb up from the ground and the night would be whole. A feeble little Christmas tree blinked in the reflection of the window. Construction paper ornaments. No glass.

That's when the alarm went off. I laughed aloud and slapped the sink with my hand. Chucky had slipped through the south door. At this very moment I could picture him running up and down the dead-end stairway looking for an outside exit that didn't exist. Just an empty set of stairs, locked, dark, and cold like Chucky's little heart. He was trapped, framed, caught in the misdemeanor of running. Poor sucker.

The staff supervisor in the kitchen left the back office and walked towards the floor. Everybody loves an alarm. We're all ambulance chasers at heart. He closed the door behind him and left me alone. I turned off the water, dried my hands and opened the window. A blast of frigid air hit me. I was glad that I'd worn my hoodie. Yeah, I got it back. I slipped on Angel's jacket with the bright Cliggett City B. I eased myself over the sink and slipped with a smile through the window. The pale-yellow walls of the kitchen were warm, sweaty with dishwater. The smell of pork chops and dish soap followed me as I dropped from the window onto the lawn. No screens. I eased the window shut and trotted off between two frozen bushes and a chain link fence. Against the horizon were the lights from scattered farms.

64

Hot chocolate splashed over the lip of the Styrofoam cup. I used my finger to smear the words "Merry Christmas Dumb Ass" on the table. The dumb ass was meant for me. The dumb ass was for everyone in the system. For Chucky. For Lyle. For Nancy. For dipshits everywhere. I folded the Pullet County letter into my jacket pocket, tossed the envelope towards the trash can. It missed and bounced to a shelf of toilet paper.

Smarty's Gas Stop had small booths along the front window, and I'd taken one in the hopes of catching a ride. Two semis and a delivery van had driven in, but I hadn't bothered to move. That's another reason I was a dumbass. I'd buried my nose in one of those hot rod magazines with the girls in bikinis, but I wasn't even looking. In my mind I was back home in Gator's GTO, watching for Beth, in love with Rita, waiting for Nancy to grow up. Across the parking lot, a long black pasture stretched to Spencer, then beyond to the horizon. The lights from the second floor glittered. By now, the staff would have realized that I'd run, slipped out the window with the pork chop grease. I wiggled my toes. They were iced like popsicles, and all one flavor—toe jam.

I smeared more hot chocolate and wrote Merry Christmas

again. This time in cursive and I underlined "Dumbass" in big swirling arcs. The door opened and I heard the squelch of a radio. A cop walked in, spoke to the cashier. They both laughed. I slumped behind the magazine and stared at my boots. And that's when it hit me, these were my boots, not my dad's. They were mine, loosened by use, conforming to the fit of my feet, not his. Something I hadn't figured out yet, almost made sense.

The cop looked me over, then walked behind the toilet paper display, and into the "Employees Only" restroom. I slid the magazine back on the rack, sipped my hot chocolate as nonchalantly as possible. I walked to the front of the store, said "Merry Christmas" to the cashier, and stepped outside. The highway stretched both ways into darkness.

The wind had picked up, a hint of sleet nipped my face from the north. I tied my hoodie closer around my neck and buttoned the top of Angel's jacket. Still the wind cut. I stood under the fluorescent lights of the canopy. It was like my boots were stuck. The lights circled around me, a ring. At any moment, I expected somebody to jump into the circle and give me a forearm to the chest, the loneliness, the harassment back at Spencer, the cold highway back to Cliggett City. A ward of the state.

No matter which way I turned there was the circle, shoulders, helmets, forearms ready to knock me on my ass. No matter which way I turned, I was still the Bull in the Ring. The way out was a one-on-one. I tried to keep my balance, but my head was spinning. I took a deep breath and leaned wearily against the hood of the police car. Warmth from the engine seeped into the back of my legs like an electric blanket. The cop came out of the bathroom and rounded the potato chip rack. I watched him buy a Snickers and refill a soft drink into a plastic cup the size of a trash tub. I slurped my hot chocolate. The cop walked towards the door. He was young, scrub-faced, built like a tight end.

"What's up?" he said.

A voice in my brain yelled, "Run for the highway," but I didn't. I sat back on the hood of the car and cleared my eyes.

"Reality," I said.

The cop almost smiled. "Sometimes," he said. "Sometimes it's up."

I shivered. Pulled my jacket to my chin.

"Supposed to get really cold tonight," he said. "First snow."

I nodded, sipped my drink.

"You alone?" he asked.

"Always," I said.

The cop glanced across the fields towards Spencer. "You from up there?"

I stared into my cup at the cooling chocolate.

"Not originally," I said.

He pulled his keys out of his jacket pocket. An amused glint in his eyes.

"Who is?" He said, "How about now?"

I finished my drink. It was cold. "That's what I'm trying to figure out."

"That's a tough one."

"Uh huh," I said. "It's a decision." I pulled the crumpled letter from my pocket. "It says here I've got two homes. One in Pittsburg. One in Cliggett City."

"That's good, right?"

"Another question. I was thinking about Nashville."

"I prefer classic rock," he said. "But Nashville has both country and western. Old joke."

"New to me."

"Know what? Both beat a cold highway."

The cop eased himself into the driver's seat. Loosened the collar on his coat.

I watched him slip his keys into the ignition, snow thickening on the windshield. He sat with his hands on the steering wheel. I knew he was waiting for me to make a decision.

"What can I do to help?" he said, cracking the window.

I ground the first ice into the sidewalk with the toe of my boot. Blue, then red, then blue again in the flickering neon. "Can you give me a lift back up the hill?"

There's a future
waiting under tomorrow's snow.
I can almost guess
the shapes, buried tricycles,
skateboards, broken
geranium planters.
Cat tracks lead up
onto a porch
with a door that almost
closes, almost latches
with a chain. Even
when slammed,
it opens.

Acknowledgments

As a poet, who cut his teeth on haiku, I found writing a novel daunting. I realized that although much is written alone with characters and plot lines banging around in my brain, I was not as isolated as I felt. Several people have gone out of their way during the writing of *Bull in the Ring* to show their support for the project and to offer insightful criticism and suggestions. First, I'd like to thank my wife Sherri who read and reread each of the many forms that *Bull in the Ring* took. Her patience with me when I lacked confidence was a steady force to keep the story moving forward. She handled her suggestions like a true English teacher, criticism followed by praise.

In the early stages of Danny's journey, my sister Jennifer Tavernaro and my daughter Karissa Reeves read the earliest draft of *Bull in the Ring*. They believed in the story in its roughest form. Others involved in the working and reworking of this novel were Blane Reeves, Wes Middleton, Theresa Middleton, Tyler Allen, Lauren Allen, Staci Chapman, Jordan Chapman, and Emilie Moll. Also, I'd like to give a shout out to Skip McConnell, John Laflen, Terry Collins, Mike Hogard, Tom Burns, Wayne Bockelman, Adam Jameson, Dana Cope, Trent Stern, James Ortolani, Jenny Ortolani, Debbie Grimaldi, Gary Grimaldi, Dianna Holman, Mike Holman, and Bobby Tavernaro. They were at the heart of the story. Special thanks to Ava Middleton, Rider Middleton, and Jack Reeves for touching the story as teenagers, and for Jude Chapman, Lyla Chapman, and Luke Allen for the future. And finally, to Stanley, who prances.

I want to give a warm thank you to Melissa Fite Johnson for her painstaking copyediting and invaluable insights into the arc of Danny's story. She was a godsend. Also, to Tracy Million Simmons who as editor, owner, and publisher of Meadowlark Press took a chance with a first novel, her professional leadership and understanding of the publishing process was exactly what I needed. I thank you both.

Cover blurbs were written by Melissa Fite Johnson, J.T. Knoll, Michael D. Graves, Julie A. Sellers, and Brian Daldorph. Their comments were humbling and gracious, understanding that *Bull in the Ring* was not just about football.

Al Ortolani is the Manuscript Editor for Woodley Press in Topeka, Kansas, and has directed a memoir writing project for Vietnam veterans across Kansas in association with the Library of Congress and Humanities Kansas. He is a 2019 recipient of the Rattle Chapbook Series Award. He has been a Kansas Notable Book recipient in 2017 and 2021. His poetry has appeared in Ted Kooser's *American Life in Poetry* and in Garrison Keillor's *Writer's Almanac*. After forty-three years of teaching English in public schools, he currently lives a life without bells and fire drills in the Kansas City area with his wife Sherri and their rescue dog Stanley.

Meadowlark FICTION

Books are a way to explore, connect, and discover. Reading gives us the gift of living lives and gaining experiences beyond our own. Publishing books is our way of saying—

We love these words,
we want to play a role in preserving them,
and we want to help share them with the world.

EXPLORE MEADOWLARK YA FICTION!

Ann Of Sunflower Lane by Julie A. Sellers

Fifteen-year-old Ann Alwyn doesn't have much choice: It's live with the maternal grandparents she's never met or go to a foster home. As Ann integrates herself into the fabric of life at Sunflower Lane, her notions of home, family, friendship, and love are broadened, but when she uncovers a difficult truth about her past, the consequences could be life-altering.

ISBN (print) 978-1-956578-23-2
ISBN (Ebook) 978-1-956578-24-9

Opulence, Kansas by Julie Stielstra

When Katie's aunt and uncle offer an escape for the summer to their Kansas farm, Katie abandons her Chicago Gold Coast high-rise life to land beneath the wider skies of the prairie. Grappling with loss and disillusionment, Katie must forge new skills and new friendships in a small town called Opulence, a town holding secrets and riches she will need before she can return home.

ISBN (print) 978-1-7342477-0-1
ISBN (Ebook) 978-1-7342477-1-8

Meadowlark Press
— since 2014 —
meadowlarkbookstore.com

www.ingramcontent.com/pod-product-compliance
Lightning Source LLC
Chambersburg PA
CBHW040224170726
48295CB00014B/801